WHAT PEOPLE ARE SAYING ABOUT

THE SPIRIT TRAP

A haunting tale that will grip the older reader as well as the young adult. It carries you through the different timeframes with elegant ease. Fascinating, well written and mind opening. Such a refreshing change from vampires.
Judy Hall, author of *The Crystal Bibles* and *Crystal Prescriptions*

Spellbinding!
Linda Davies, New York Times bestselling author of *Nest of Vipers, Ark Storm, the children's Djinn Quartet*, and many others

The alarming screech of a peacock plunges Tatania into a puzzle that is perhaps hers: a previous life in revolutionary France. Veryan Williams Wynn has crafted a great tale – part mystery, part thriller, part ghost story, as two cousins struggle to make sense of hauntings, apparitions, sudden chills and the fate of ancestors who need to be freed from the spirit trap.

Along with Tatania and her stalwart cousin Marcus, we follow clues leading to a mysterious French Chateau, snowbound labyrinths and the bony depths of the catacombs deep beneath the streets of Paris. *The Spirit Trap* is a great yarn and a page turner for young adults and adults alike.
Murray Morrison, author of *Time Sphere*

The Spirit Trap

The Spirit Trap

Veryan Williams-Wynn

LODESTONE BOOKS

Winchester, UK
Washington, USA

First published by Lodestone Books, 2015
Lodestone Books is an imprint of John Hunt Publishing Ltd., Laurel House, Station Approach, Alresford, Hants, SO24 9JH, UK
office1@jhpbooks.net
www.johnhuntpublishing.com

For distributor details and how to order please visit the 'Ordering' section on our website.

ISBN: 978 1 78535 074 0
Library of Congress Control Number: 2015934350

A CIP catalogue record for this book is available from the British Library.

Passages from 'The Listeners' by kind permission of the Literary Trustees of Walter de la Mare and the Society of Authors as their representative.

Design: Stuart Davies

Printed and bound in the USA by Edwards Brothers Malloy

CONTENTS

For

Charles, Alexi, Lucy and Robert.

Chapter 1

Threads of the Tapestry

Tatiana glanced over her shoulder for the third time in as many minutes. She couldn't help it; the eerie rustling as she scrunched through the dried leaves carpeting the damp mossy-smelling earth was making her jittery. She rubbed her arms and shuddered, was it just a wintery chill or the unnatural cold she felt whenever … no, surely she'd be safe from ghosts out here? She needed to concentrate, focus on the poem she was supposed to be learning for school and forget about the picture and the inexplicable goings-on in the drawing room. Praying it was just the cold, not some unseen presence in the garden playing tricks, she stopped chewing her lip, crossed her fingers and began to recite.

'"Is there anybody there?" said the traveller,
knocking on the moonlit door;
While his … no… And *his horse*?'

'Which is it?' said Tatiana, struggling to remember the lines. Thrusting her hands deeper into her pockets, she paced backwards and forwards until coming to a patch of dappled sunlight filtering through the overhanging branches. There she released her hair from its clip and shook it loose allowing the sun to form splashes of russet on the wild, unruly mass spilling over her shoulders; *if only it was always this wicked foxy red instead of its usual boring auburn colour.* Tatiana tossed her hair back from her face and frowned, her mind searching for the words she was trying to memorize for homework.

'And his horse in the silence champ'd…'

'Hey! I think I've nearly got it.'

'Is there anybody there?' she shouted to the wind, and flinging her arms out wide, spun around like a windmill.

She stopped spinning and sensing a slight movement, cocked her head, listening. She looked around half expecting to see her mum, but there was no sign of her and as far as she could see nothing other than herself was disturbing the hazy winter's afternoon.

'Where was I?' she muttered, leaning her back against the gnarled bark of a sprawling cherry tree. 'Oh yes...'

'Is there anybody there? he...'

Her sentence remained unfinished, as a prolonged mewing-shriek filled the air. Momentarily, Tatiana froze before cowering to the ground. Without knowing why, she found herself making the sign of the cross over and over again. *Oh, God*! *What was that*? She wanted to run, but her legs had turned to jelly and wouldn't move. Swallowing hard she squeezed her eyes into slits and stayed where she was, crouched amongst the exposed tree roots. After several silent minutes had passed, she uncurled just enough to make a surreptitious survey of the seemingly empty garden. *Dare she make a run for it*?

She was getting shakily to her feet when another shriek pierced the air, this time coming quite distinctly from the bushes behind the cherry tree. 'Please, whoever you are, go away,' she whispered. Beads of sweat were forming on her ashen face, but she daren't move. Instead she shrank back onto the dank ground shielding her head with her folded arms.

Whatever could have produced such a terrifying noise? It sounded like someone being tortured, and there most certainly was *'somebody there'*.

A rustling in the dry leaves beneath the camellias made her turn; seeing nothing, she decided to make her escape, but as she stood up a head shot out from between the shiny leaves, its button-black eyes staring directly at her. Slowly she turned to confront the intruder and watched as the strange blue face with black and white markings topped with an upstanding crest of feathers advanced towards her. The head, attached to a blue snake-like neck, became more and more elongated until the body emerged from the undergrowth.

Tatiana released her breath with an exaggerated whoosh. 'After all that you're just a bird!' What on earth was a peacock doing here? Seemingly oblivious to her, the intruder shook out its feathers and strutted away, its trailing tail sweeping a path through the leaves. She was still staring at the retreating bird, when it looked back and their eyes locked.

'*Tati! Tatiana*! Where are you?' Her mum's heavily accented voice was accompanied by the sound of her footsteps pounding along the path to the hidden garden. '*Tatiana*!'

'I'm here, by the cherry tree,' she shouted, as her mum, hair flying in all directions rounded the corner.

'Are you all right?' she gasped. 'I heard you scream.'

'No I didn't, it did,' said Tatiana, pointing at the peacock.

'Goodness! Whatever's that doing here?'

'Don't know. It just appeared out of the bushes.'

'That's strange,' said her mum. 'I didn't know anyone in the village kept peacocks.'

'Well it can't stay here,' said Tatiana giving the bird a baleful look.

'Why ever not?' said her mum, moving closer to the creature. 'It has the most fabulous feathers I've ever seen. Think how lovely they'd be on a hat, or I could make them in—'

'Mum!'

'Only the ones that drop out! I'm not about to pluck it!'

Tatiana continued staring at the bird unaware that her knuckles had turned white or that her nails were making sharp indentations in the soft cover of her schoolbook. Mystified as to why she should be so nervous, she turned slowly to her mum and in a shuddering voice, whispered, 'It gives me the creeps.'

'You can't be scared of such a magnificent creature, Tati, you're fourteen not four and you know perfectly well it won't hurt you.'

'I'm not frightened of *it* exactly … but there's something sinister about it that I really *don't like,*' she said, lowering her voice.

'Well I expect it will fly back to wherever it came from,' said her mum, giving her a reassuring kiss on the forehead before wandering off.

Tatiana continued to watch the bird as it scratched amongst the fallen leaves, but even from a safe distance it put her on edge. Why should she be so rattled by a bird? It couldn't be because of its size and it seemed pretty harmless; her mum was right, the way its bright blue feathers shimmered in the sun was quite amazing and reminded her of dragonflies she'd seen with her cousin Marcus in the summer.

'What *is it* about you?' she asked, shaking her head. She was about to leave the garden when the bird strutted towards her, drew back its head and let out another high-pitched *eeeooowwww* right in her face.

Later that evening, the incident of the peacock behind her, Tatiana sat at the piano in the drawing room, her hands flying up and down the keys, practising for her lesson the following day. Yes! She'd got it. No problem there then, but she wasn't so sure about her English homework.

'I'll see if I can recite the poem for you,' she said turning to the woman in the picture hanging on the wall behind her. Tatiana looked at the gilt-framed portrait of her ancestor, the beautiful Isabella Lafont. It was a picture she'd known all her life, although until recently it had hung in her grandparents' apartment in Paris and had only come to England after her grandmother Natasha's death. Her grandfather had insisted on her mum taking it away at once, along with the urn containing her grandmother's ashes. Tatiana loved the picture almost as much as she'd loved her grandmother. The eighteenth-century artist's style and detail fascinated her, if only she could paint like that! But what she admired most was the woman's sky-blue silk dress with its wide pink sash and lace-edged sleeves. It was so beautiful; though she couldn't quite imagine wearing, let alone *running* in, such a long skirt! She was so intrigued by Isabella that she frequently found herself chatting out loud to her, as if she was actually there in the room with her.

She'd decided to make up a tune for the poem; singing the words would make them easier to remember. Tatiana picked out a simple melody and began to hum. She was getting on well and focussing on the final verses when her mum stuck her head around the door.

'There's a film on television I think you'd enjoy, why don't you come and watch it?'

Tatiana didn't look up. 'Can't,' she said. 'I'm doing my homework.'

'Doesn't look much like it to me, tinkering about on the piano. It's set during the French Revolution, the same period that Isabella lived, so it might interest you.'

'This is homework! I'm learning a poem—'

'Come on, you can finish it later, besides, you can't stay in here, it's freezing. The heating must have gone wrong,' her mum said, and pulling her cardigan tightly around herself, went to check the radiator. 'How peculiar, it's hot! Have you opened the window?'

'Of course not, Mum. Haven't you noticed, it's nearly always cold in here these days?'

'Not until now,' she said.

'It's been like this ever since the picture and granny's ashes arrived. Sometimes the cold swirls around the room and I get a weird sensation like icy fingers running down my back ... if I ignore it, it prods me!'

'Tati! *Stop it!*'

'Well it's *much* worse than goose bumps. *And* I can feel someone watching me. I think it's the picture, Isabella's eyes follow me, like they're pleading ... I think it's ... her ghost.'

'Don't be ridiculous, it's nothing but your imagination!' her mum said, hurrying to the door, but Tatiana couldn't help noticing how she glanced sideways at the picture as she went by.

'It's just the way the artist painted the eyes that gives the impression of them following you,' she said. 'And remind me to get the heating fixed tomorrow.'

'Mum!' But it was no use, her mum just didn't get it; didn't believe the cold could be caused by something she could neither see nor name.

'Come on, the film will soon dispel all this nonsense.'

'*Have I got to*?'

'Yes. It's a great Dickens classic.'

Tatiana followed her mum to the cosy snug and slumped onto a creaky leather beanbag in front of the television where a drama with people dressed in eighteenth-century costume was playing.

'What's this?' asked Tatiana scowling. 'It's not even in colour!'

'Well it is quite old,' said her mum. 'It's *A Tale of Two Cities*, and probably made in the nineteen fifties.'

'You must be joking! No way I'm watching this.'

'It's a good story, at least give it a try.'

Tatiana let out an exaggerated sigh and crossing her arms, wriggled deeper into the shifting beans. She'd watch the film till the next advert to please her mum, then go back to her poem.

Her mum was right. The ladies with their high powdered wigs and floor-sweeping gowns were of exactly the same period as the portrait next door. It was only because of the picture that she had a vague interest in the French Revolution, but she knew very little about it other than a whole load of people, mainly aristocrats, had their heads cut off. Here, for the first time, the reality of those turbulent years was being revealed in all its gory detail. She watched as innocent people lost their heads to the hated guillotine and was so absorbed in the story that it wasn't until a peacock outside a chateau let out a screech that she was brought back to reality. Tatiana jumped, and covering her ears, cast a bewildered look at her mum.

'That's done it!' she cried, and scrambling awkwardly out of the beanbag, hurtled from the room. She was standing in the passage, wondering whether to go back, when she overheard her parents talking about her.

'Whatever's the matter with Tatiana?' she heard her dad say. *Oh no! He sounded irritated, why? What had she done to annoy him this time?*

'I've no idea, she doesn't usually get upset by films, but she has become rather over-sensitive recently,' said her mum. 'She even wanted to move the piano out of the drawing room, until I pointed out there was nowhere else for it to go.'

'What did she want to do that for?

'She thinks she's being watched…'

'Watched? Who by exactly?'

Tatiana shot back to the drawing room and was staring at the piano when her mum came in. 'What's wrong, Tati?'

'It's those horrible birds, I can't stand them,' she said, trying to stop her voice from quavering.

'But they're so beautiful … and it's only a film.'

'It's not them, it's the noise they make.'

'I know it's not very nice, but it's nothing to be frightened of,' she said, putting an arm around her. 'Come back or you'll miss the end.'

Wrapping her arms around her mum, Tatiana glanced at the portrait. *She really didn't understand why she was scared, and of what exactly? A noise?*

This time she curled up on the sofa beside her mum, and watched the remainder of the film clutching a cushion to her chest. All went well until she saw a young girl, who she judged to be about fourteen, like herself, climb the steps of the scaffold and kneel at the feet of the executioner. The girl's brimming eyes were fixed on his black-hooded face pleading for mercy, but at a signal from him, she rapidly made the sign of the cross, and bent forward placing her slender neck on the blood-stained block. When Tatiana heard the swish of the falling blade followed by a dull thud, an icy tremor swept over her.

'How *could they*?' she cried. 'She was no older than me!' and dropping the cushion on the floor, rushed out of the room. Taking the stairs two at a time, she bolted to her bedroom and flung herself face down on the bed.

Tatiana found it difficult to sleep. Fragments of her tune, a persistent repetition of '*is anybody there*?' from the poem, muddled echoes of the peacock and images of people being beheaded, kept revolving through her mind, which, although not so frightening in themselves, combined to fill her with an inexplicable dread. Then she remembered the girl in the film making the sign of the cross before being guillotined, just like she'd done in the garden; strange. *It's not as though she was catholic or even particularly religious, how weird was that?* And so she continued to toss and turn, until her beloved cat, Pushkin, jumped onto the bed. That was better; she pulled her under the covers, hugging her soft warmth until a rumbling purr lulled her into a fitful, dream-filled sleep.

Where was she? She appeared to be in a long narrow corridor formed of tightly clipped hedges so high they reached far above her head. Looking up she saw how the lowering sun was edging the uppermost leaves in a coral glow in stark contrast to the deep indigo shadows where she stood. She seemed to be trapped in a vast maze and wasn't sure she liked it, but propelled by curiosity she set off along the path. Almost immediately she came to a T-junction. Which way? Left or right? Whatever she chose, she'd inevitably arrive at either a dead end or another similar junction. Tatiana hurried on, continuously twisting and turning, but no matter how hard she tried she couldn't find the middle, nor could she find her way out. She was beginning to panic and longing for the dream to end, when she heard music.

Could this be a clue? With renewed hope she set off in pursuit of the sound only to meet yet another hedge blocking her way. 'I can't get out! Please help me,' she yelled.

'This is how life is,' said a disembodied voice. 'The whole of life is a question of choices.'

'Well how am I supposed to know which is the right one?' she asked. It answered in a mocking voice. 'You aren't, that would make it too easy, pointless in your being here, in being born; trust yourself and follow your instincts.'

She was pondering this strange statement when she heard the music again and although the words were indistinct, she could tell it was a young girl singing.

'Who's there?' she called. The singing immediately stopped. 'I know you're there,' she shouted, swivelling on the wet gravel. '*Please* help me find the way out.'

But the silence remained leaden and the chill air swirling through the maze did nothing to ease her sense of foreboding. With the sound of scrunching gravel ringing in her ears, she ran to the next junction where she caught a glimpse of the girl. '*Wait*!' she cried, sprinting after the retreating figure, but upon reaching the next bend all she saw was a disappearing flash of blue velvet. Then she heard the girl singing again, and this time the words were clear. The girl was singing in French.

'*Hey!* That's my tune!' Tatiana shouted. 'But you're singing the wrong words!'

She set off again, slowly and calmly, this time letting her intuition guide her. As she followed the ebb and flow of the notes, she caught occasional glimpses of the elusive blue cloak and in what seemed like no time, was out of the maze. Free at last, she was enjoying the warmth of the final rays of the setting sun when the sound of a peacock calling nearby made her jump. The sound reverberated around in her head until evaporating into the descending dusk, when to her dismay she looked up to find herself back amongst the imprisoning hedges.

'How can this be? I was out a moment ago.'

She ran frantically twisting and turning this way and that as a childishly high-pitched voice taunted, 'See, you can't get out, you will *never* escape; not until you've solved the riddle and saved your maman, will *you* escape!'

Tatiana ran and ran trying to get away from the voice, but no matter which way she turned, she couldn't get rid of it. 'You have to reach the *centre* of *you*, know yourself for who *you* are, only then will you both be free.'

Tatiana awoke screaming. *Oh god!* She groped under the bedclothes, seeking the comfort of a reassuring purr from Pushkin, but even that didn't help. *What a load of rubbish; why did she have to save her mum? What from? Her dad? Surely not.* She decided to dismiss the dream as one of the gobbledygook sort, which if like most dreams, would soon be forgotten.

Chapter 2

Enlisting Marcus's Help

The following morning, Tatiana, unable to get the dream from her mind, watched her mum as she prepared breakfast. She seemed her normal cheerful self, if anything too cheerful for so early in the morning, especially to Tatiana after a bad night.

'You okay, Mum?'

'Me? Absolutely, why don't I look all right?' she asked turning to check her face in the kitchen mirror.

'You look fine. I was just wondering ... and Dad? He seemed really grumpy last night.'

'Oh don't worry about him, I expect he was just anxious about today's auction in London – he's desperate to buy a picture for a client and it's been generating far too much interest for his liking,' she said.

Well Mum seemed okay and as far as she could tell, didn't need saving from anything, least of all Dad, so why the horrible dream? If it was still bugging her when she got back from school she'd phone Marcus.

Marcus, and Tatiana had known each other all of their lives; had played together since early childhood and were such close friends that they were often taken for siblings. This was partially on account of their dads being cousins, but also because of the strong bond between the two families. Marcus, who was two years older than her, was like an older brother, and the one person who Tatiana trusted more than anyone. With him she had no secrets, and if anyone could help her make sense of her dream he would – that was if she could get hold of him at his posh boarding school.

Tatiana returned from school and had gone to the drawing room to practise her music assignment when she heard a crash accompanied by a truncated meow coming from the direction of the back hall. *What was that?* She shot out to the passage and was looking around when she noticed the cellar door was open. *Oh No! Pushkin must* be *down there.* She shuddered; she just hated the cellars.

Even on the hottest of summer days the cellars were cold with an ever-present musty smell of damp stone. A smell so hostile that it made her want to hold her nose rather than inhale. The cellar door, under the back stairs, was opened by a key that only worked from the outside. She pushed the door further open and fumbled for the light switch at the top of the stone steps.

'Pushkin?' she called, but there was no response other than a muffled clink from below. 'Pushkin?' Suppose she was hurt? She'd have to go down.

Treading carefully past a pile of newspapers stacked on the first step and skirting the empty bottles lined up on another, she made her way to the bottom. The surrounding slate floor was littered with empty boxes, thrown down from above, where they'd stay until her mum took them to the re-cycling centre in town along with the bottles and papers.

The cellars consisted of two rows of small vaults either side of a central passageway. Some were lined with shelves, others partitioned into bays where, in days gone by, large quantities of wine would have been stored, but now contained no more than a half-dozen cardboard boxes with an assortment of what her dad called 'kitchen plonk'. She wasn't interested in her dad's wine, she just wanted to find Pushkin and get out. She'd nearly reached the end of the passage, when the cellars were suddenly plunged into darkness.

'Turn the lights on!' she shouted, and tripping over the silent Pushkin, fell, knocking her head against the wall.

The darkness swirled silently around her, as if bats circled overhead, and her stomach convulsed at the overpowering stench rising from the ground. As she pulled herself upright, the ground squelching beneath her, made her gag. *'Odd's Fish!'* She heard someone mumble. She was still clutching her stomach, when she heard the voice again. *'Surely we will add our own puke to these festering mounds of excrement covering the floor?'* Then all the horrors of some unknown, yet unforgettable past welled up in the darkness surrounding her.

Tatiana opened her eyes with a start. *What on earth was that?* Feeling Pushkin by her feet, she grabbed her and stumbled towards a faint strip of light edging the door, groped her way up the stairs, and finding the door unlocked, was out. She banged the door shut behind her and leant back, shuddering. *That was just horrible and so weird – where had that strange voice and unbelievable smell come from?*

She had to ring Marcus. She looked at her watch; with any luck he'd have finished his evening studies by now.

'Hi, Marcus … I need to talk to you, properly, not on the phone, and was wondering if—'

'Hey, funny you should ring I was just trying to decide what do when I break up for the Christmas holidays. Mum and Dad are busy the first weekend and although I've been asked to stay with a friend, I'd much rather see you. Could I come and stay?'

Tatiana sighed; just knowing he was coming made her feel instantly better.

Two days later, Tatiana was on her hands and knees in the drawing room kowtowing before Isabella's picture. She'd started performing this strange ritual after seeing a film with Marcus in which a Chinese family had honoured their ancestors by prostrating themselves in front of their portraits. Later Marcus had jokingly pressed his hands together, knelt and bowed to the portrait of her ancestor, which had led Tatiana to make a habit of doing the same; something that drove her dad crazy. 'Get up off the floor, Tatiana,' he'd shout. 'What do you think you're doing, you're not bloody Chinese!'

She was still on her knees, staring up at Isabella, when she heard a soft fluttering behind her. She turned expecting to see a trapped moth, but instead saw a page from her music book, propped open on the piano, turn over by itself. Thinking there must be a window open she checked, but no – they were all closed. Then she watched as page after page quivered and flipped over as if turned by an unseen hand. She jumped up and was staring at the piano when the book juddered violently and fell to the floor at her feet.

'Oh my God!' she gasped and crumpled onto the piano stool. She was trying to collect her scattered thoughts when, noticing out of the corner of her eye, a misty shape blurring the fireplace, she spun around, but too late, it had gone. Tatiana leapt up and with faltering steps, crossed to the fireplace, where, with a show of bravado she didn't feel, she confronted the silver cup containing her grandmother's ashes. '*Did* you do that? Or was it you?' she said glancing reproachfully at Isabella's unresponsive face. 'Whoever's playing these tricks, please stop it.'

Tatiana retreated to the relative safety of her bedroom. The trouble was that their house was anything but normal, partly because it was very old and rambling, but also on account of her dad dealing in antiques. Every room in the house was crammed full of random objects and dilapidated furniture he'd bought at auction and was waiting to restore or sell. Even her bedroom was furnished with strange objects, including a stringless, once gilded harp, which she quite liked, and the more recent addition of a moth-eaten tapestry, which, convinced it must harbour untold numbers of spiders, she didn't.

She threw herself onto her bed, her pulse still racing, her palms clammy and with a buzzing sensation in her limbs. If only she could see who or whatever '*it*' was in the drawing room, then she'd know whether to be frightened or not. She grabbed a cushion and hugging it tight to the hard knot in the pit of her stomach, slumped back on her pillows staring vacantly at the wall. The weekend couldn't come soon enough.

Each evening that week saw her slip warily into the brooding silence of the drawing room. The hairs on her arms, acting as a barometer to any suggestion of a whispering draught, warned her when the temperature was about to drop; then, her fingers would take on the rhythm of her quickening breath and she'd play in a torrent of urgency and fumbled notes. Occasionally a fleeting touch on the shoulder would make her stop. She'd go rigid, fingers splayed mid-movement as she held her breath, waiting. Until, unable to bear the suspense a moment longer, she'd wheel around hoping to see something tangible, something she could confront, but there was never anything there, least nothing she could see.

At last it was Friday and the start of the Christmas holidays. While waiting for Marcus to arrive, she'd been helping her mum with the Christmas decorations. He'd said they'd be there by three o'clock, but she had a niggling feeling that they wouldn't.

'Bet there's an accident and they'll be late,' she'd said, twisting a garland of ivy and pine through the banisters rails.

'Don't be silly,' her mum had replied tersely.

'We'll see,' muttered Tatiana. And much to her mum's disquiet, she was right, and it was gone six by the time they arrived.

'Sorry we're late,' exclaimed Marcus, leaping out of the car.

'An accident on the motorway, I'm afraid,' said his mum.

Tatiana greeted Marcus with a huge hug. 'You've grown,' she whispered. She didn't remember him being so much taller than her in the summer. And he'd changed, only she wasn't too sure how, difficult to tell. His face was definitely thinner, but it was more than that – as if he'd suddenly grown up. Or was it just because he was wearing a shirt under his jumper instead of the usual tee shirt? Whatever it was, he had a more together look, but then perhaps that was how they dressed at his school. Once he'd dumped his bags in the spare room, she took him off to the old barn of a playroom where they settled down in the saggy, springless armchairs for a catch-up.

'I'm so glad to see your dad hasn't sold your rocking horse,' he said, glancing at the wooden horse dominating the room.

'No, well you know what he's like, never sells anything much, besides I'm determined to keep it—' she was saying, when Marcus stopped her.

'Tati! What have you done to yourself?'

'Oh, it's nothing much ... I fell over in the cellars ... I don't remember exactly what happened, it was all rather strange,' she said, fingering the grazed lump on the side of her forehead.

'Strange? Like what?'

After she'd told him about the incident in the cellar she asked him what he thought.

'Are you sure you weren't knocked out, even for a couple of seconds and dreamt the grotty stuff and wanting to be sick?'

'I don't think so, but then why did I say "puke"?' I never use that word nor would I have imagined shitty grot all over the floor ... although once I'd come to my senses, like I *had* been knocked out, I realised that the stink of sewage had gone, and, well, there isn't any other explanation.'

He nodded. 'Is this what you wanted to talk about?'

'Yes and no, because when I rang, I wanted to ask you about a dream which was bugging me, only since then there's been all this other stuff happening.'

'Where do you want to begin?'

'Difficult to say,' she said, 'because there was more than just the dream, something else happened ... to do with a peacock.'

'A peacock, Tati! Was it displaying its tail like it fancied you?' he asked, and unexpectedly blushing, turned away, hoping she hadn't noticed. For an awkward moment neither said a thing.

'No,' she said, peering quizzically at him through her eyelashes. 'And don't be so mean, it really scared me, not the bird, it was okay, but the noise it made. Then I watched a film on TV with Mum and when a peacock appeared, I ... it was so stupid, but I got really upset.'

'That's not like you,' he said, shaking his head. 'You normally only go mushy over sloppy stuff.'

'I know. Then ... well, I'll begin at the beginning...'

When she was coming to the end Marcus leant forward. 'So you were being persecuted by the noise?'

'Yes, but that's not all, it got worse. As the dream was ending, I was told I had to rescue my mum or else!'

'Rescue your mum?!'

'Yes, which doesn't make sense, but then worse things keep happening ... when I'm awake...' She could feel herself starting to shake; even thinking about the drawing room made her nervous and feeling her throat tightening, she hesitated, she didn't want to get all stupid and emotional in front of Marcus.

'Bit weird, but then maybe there's a connection, like it's linked to something you can't remember, something that happened in the past.'

'Do you mean in another lifetime?'

'I don't see why not. Don't you ever wonder if we've lived before, and if so, whether what happened then might influence what we do now?'

The increasingly puzzled expression on Tatiana's face slowly relaxed. 'That's such an exciting idea, and you really think my fear of peacocks might be from ... some other time?'

'Why not? If the sound's frightening for no logical reason, then maybe you had a bad experience related to it.'

'Must have been pretty terrible if it scares me so much.'

'Perhaps you were killed by a peacock!'

Tatiana rolled her eyes at such a daft idea, but crazy as it was, Marcus's remark continued to whirl through her mind. *If he was right, and it was a memory from a previous life, then she needn't be afraid, nor would she have to rescue her mum after all. What a relief!*

'Hardly likely, but then everything was really getting to me so I looked up dreaming ... and stuff on the internet and it was amazing what I found.'

'What exactly?'

'Well, for a start it's possible to manipulate dreams, make things happen – lucid dreaming it's called. And then there was all this stuff about Ancient Egyptian priests using dreams as part of their training to become psychics, and I wondered if I could train myself like that?'

'To be psychic?'

'Yes, you see ... oh, it's nothing,' she said changing her mind.

'Sounds like dreams used to be really important back then.'

'I think they still are, and with my maze dream bugging me so much I now write mine down every night hoping it might help with ... you know.'

Marcus's eyes narrowed as Tatiana started shredding a tissue. 'No, Tati, I don't know, and if you want me to help, then you'd better tell me everything.'

Tatiana lowered her eyes and nodded. It was impossible to hide anything from Marcus; he was too perceptive, always honest and upfront, so no matter who you were, you always knew exactly where you stood with him.

She cleared her throat. 'You're right there is more; something creepy is going on here. Something really frightening and I haven't a clue what it is.'

Marcus leant forward. 'Start at the beginning, Tati.'

Tatiana clasped her hands around her knees and started to talk. Marcus listened without once interrupting, occasionally nodding, encouraging her to go on until she'd told him everything there was to tell.

'...and I get this creepy sensation like cobwebs clinging to me and the feeling something I can't see is trying to force me to ... I don't know what, but it won't give up! Yesterday, when I was playing the piano, something pulled my hair. I shouted at it to stop, and it did, but it didn't go away; instead it made the lights flicker on and off 'til I thought I'd scream. Do you think it's Granny's ashes causing it, or, but it sounds so stupid ... *the picture*?'

Marcus looked puzzled, and running his hands through his hair, said, 'No way could a picture do those things, and why would your grandmother's spirit want to stick around a heap of old ash? Yet it does sound like someone's trying to get your attention, but what on earth for?' Seeing Tatiana shiver Marcus returned to the safer topic of her grandmother. 'Are you sure you haven't seen her since she died, not even in dreams?'

She shook her head. 'I wish I could, because if it's her in the drawing room I don't need to be spooked and if it isn't ... well, I'll go crazy if it doesn't stop ... and it's not like just avoiding the drawing room, 'cos I have an important music exam coming up. Will you help me?'

Marcus shrugged. 'I'm not remotely psychic so I don't know what use I'll be.'

'Everyone feels things Marcus, even Mum felt the cold when 'it' was in the room.'

'Okay, I'll try then.'

'You will? Fantastic!' she said, throwing her arms around him.

Chapter 3

Natasha's Request

That night, Tatiana slept soundly, that was until a succession of thumps and high pitched squeaks on the landing outside her door disturbed her dreams, bringing her back to reality. Grabbing a pillow, she hurled it at the door.

'Pushkin! Leave that poor mouse alone!' she shouted.

The noise momentarily ceased. A long silence was then broken by the sound of claws scampering over bare floorboards and a soft rhythmic thumping of Pushkin going downstairs. Tatiana sighed and turning over noticed shadows moving on the wall beside her bed. She hadn't drawn the curtains, and the moon shining through the wind-blown branches of the tree outside was projecting constantly changing shapes onto the walls. Through her sleep-filled eyes she saw the shadows as dancing couples in French court dress, like that of Isabella's in the portrait. She imagined grand people exchanging remarks, the ladies flirting behind fans and laughing as they arranged secret meetings, all the while drinking and eating from tables laden with huge quantities of food on gold and silver platters. Mesmerised, she watched while the shapes merged into Isabella, not as she was in the picture, but all dirty and dishevelled in a stinking rat-infested cell and, clinging to her ragged skirts, weeping and begging to be allowed to stay, was a young girl. Tatiana, sensing the child's misery, closed her eyes, trying to blot out the chilling images.

'Tatiana?'

What was that? She strained, listening. 'Is anybody there?' she asked, but no one answered. After waiting a couple of minutes she slipped out of bed and in the process of pulling the curtains across the window thought, for a fleeting second, she saw a figure standing on the grass beneath the tree.

'Granny?' When she looked more closely all she could make out in the small patch of moonlight was an eddy of leaves whirling around the gnarled trunk. 'This is so frustrating, if that was you, why can't you talk to me?' she grumbled.

She'd stumbled back to bed and was snuggling under the covers, searching for areas of warmth with her cold feet, when she again heard something, only this time it was accompanied by an icy blast and a chill tingling down her spine, a sensation, she knew meant something *'other'* was in the room with her. Shivering, and with her teeth starting to chatter, she pulled the blankets over her chin and peered around the darkened room. As her eyes gradually adjusted to the dark, she tensed, steeling herself not to scream if anything moved or jumped out at her.

Had the whole house suddenly become haunted? Was nowhere safe anymore, not even her bedroom? With the cold air still swirling around the room, she pulled the bedclothes right over her head; she'd had more than enough of inexplicable goings-on and wanted to sleep.

'Keep your eyes shut and listen,' came a voice. The hairs on Tatiana's arms were standing on end as she grabbed her pillow and holding it tight to her ears, waited, her stomach churning in dread. Alone in a huge, dark, creaky room wasn't the moment she wanted to encounter anything, let alone ghostly voices. *Why was Pushkin off mousing when she needed her?* The silence increased in intensity until exploding in a torrent of soundless whispering in her head, when, through the jabbering, she heard the voice again. This time her whole body stiffened. *This is so not happening – it's just not possible, there's no one here but me … the voice must be inside my head*! Then, although faint and whispery, she recognised it. It was her grandmother's voice, comfortingly familiar with its unmistakable Russian accent.

'*Oh … my … God,* is … is that really you, Granny?' whispered Tatiana, her head still firmly under the bedclothes.

'Of course, Tatiana, who did you think?'

Was she asleep? Was this a dream or her imagination? Unable to tell, she slowly unblocked her ears and emerging from under the covers, peered around the dimly lit room.

'I can't see you…'

'I know. You must be patient with me, because I'm not very good at this sort of thing.'

'But you're here, speaking to me.'

'Yes, only with difficulty … it may sound as if I'm talking, but I'm not, I'm using telepathy.'

'Telepathy?'

'Yes. Communicating by thought. You think very hard about what you want to say, then the other person "hears" the thoughts, not out loud, but in their head. It's quick, has no language problems and is easy, unlike appearing physically. That I find very difficult to maintain for more than a few seconds at a time.'

Unable to see anything, Tatiana continued to stare into the darkness above her head. *If this was real, then she mustn't waste the opportunity.* 'Granny, I have to ask you something about the picture downstairs, the one that belonged to you. Ever since it arrived it's felt as if someone's watching me and strange things happen, but then your ashes are also in the room and … is it *you* haunting me?'

'No! I wouldn't do that to you, but that's also why I've come. I need to talk to you about Isabella.'

'It is her then!'

'I doubt it, because although her spirit's still around, it's stuck in France not here in England.'

'Then *who* is it in the drawing room? And *why* are they doing it?'

'I don't know … someone must be trying to attract your attention.'

'What for?'

'Probably the same reason I'm here now; to get help for her.'

'*Help!* Why does she need help?'

'Because she doesn't realise she's dead. Her spirit's stuck, unable to move on or reincarnate again.'

'You mean she's a ghost?'

'That's right. Her final months were appalling, especially immediately before her death. She was terrified and worried sick about what would become of you when she was gone … she was powerless to help herself, let alone anyone else, and that's how she's remained. Trapped by fear.'

'That's awful! So what happened to … did you say "you" just now, meaning *me*?'

'Yes, you lived then, as did I,' she said. We escaped together, you and I, but she never knew and died in torment.'

'During the Revolution?'

'Yes.'

'Was she so very bad?'

'No. Isabella was basically a good woman, but like so many of the French aristocrats in those days, horribly misguided and unaware of just how privileged and frivolous their lives were. There were many people like her who simply didn't realise how very deprived the ordinary people's existences were.'

'Was she executed?'

'I don't know for sure, but I think she probably died in prison. I was researching the family history before I became ill, but it wasn't until after I died that I discovered she was trapped... so now I'm appealing to you.'

'*Me*?'

'Yes. Only you can rescue her now, Tatiana. You *must* do it.'

'*But how can I?* She's dead and since you're dead too, why can't you help?'

'I've tried, but she doesn't respond to me. Because she thinks she's still alive, she remains very close to the earth where the vibrations are slow and dense, similar to those on earth, so like most living people, she's unaware of spirit presences, which vibrate much faster.'

'Oh no! She's been stuck for more than two hundred years!'

'Don't worry about that, time means nothing here, but she does need to be rescued, and since your vibrations are closer to hers than mine, you may succeed where I've failed.'

'How will I find her?'

'It won't be easy; get Marcus to help,' whispered her grandmother, whose voice was becoming more distant. 'It's very important you do this … and don't let "it" get to you and become ill like I did, Tati.'

'Wait! Please don't go Granny —'

But too late, she'd gone. Tatiana jolted upright and, with her senses buzzing, switched on the light and reached for her notebook.

Rain beat a steady tattoo against the windows. It had rained all morning confining Marcus and Tatiana to the playroom. Marcus was sitting at the desk idling on the computer, while Tatiana strummed her guitar.

'Since we can't investigate the "thing" in the drawing room with your mum doing decorations in there, why don't you try working on your dream, see what you can find out about peacocks?'

Tatiana looked doubtful. 'How do I do that?'

'It should be easy, close your eyes and imagine being back in the maze again, then watch, sort of like daydreaming.'

Tilting her head to one side, she blinked, and said, 'Easy?' Then seeing the dogged expression on his face said, 'Okay, I'll try, but you'll have to guide me.' She uncurled from the armchair and crossed to the rocking horse. 'If I sit here, it'll stop me falling asleep.'

In one agile movement she sprang onto the rocking horse's back, draped herself, lithe and sensuous as a sleeping leopard, along his neck, clasped her hands around his head and looked at Marcus, waiting for a signal.

'You still doing ballet?' he asked.

'Yes, I just love it, but Dad wants me to give it up.'

'Well, don't,' he said, pulling a face. 'Dancing is so ... you, Tati.'

'I know,' she said, with a long drawn-out sigh. 'But he just wants me to concentrate on boring academic subjects.'

Tatiana remained very still trying to stop her mind from rambling. *It was all very well Marcus telling her to watch, she'd been in the same position for so long her arms were numb, and still she hadn't seen a thing, let alone the maze.* 'I can't do this, absolutely nothing is happening,' she said, slipping off the horse and rubbing her shoulders.

'Well it was only an idea. But maybe we need to find something more ... no! *I've got it*! What we need is a *peacock*!' he said, as an impish grin spread across his face.

Tatiana grabbed an abandoned trainer from the floor and hurled it at Marcus.

'Easy, tiger, easy, I was only teasing,' he said, emerging, hands in the air, from behind a chair. 'I didn't know you'd be so touchy.'

Tatiana stopped glaring and mumbled, 'Sorry.'

'No worries, anyway I've found something really interesting on the internet – that exclamation you heard in the cellars when you fell over.'

'Odd's Fish?'

'Exactly! It was a favourite expression of eighteenth-century dandies, like the Scarlet Pimpernel.'

Tatiana stared at Marcus. 'Where did I get something like that from, and why?'

'Don't ask me, but what if we went to the cellars and you tried linking back to that moment, you might find out?'

Tatiana stared intently at Marcus, her eyes widening. 'Have you noticed, these things seem to be triggered by my senses ... the sounds, the smell...'

'And, unlike most people, you seem to have a sixth sense too! Come on, Tati, we're going to check out the smell – in the cellars.'

Tatiana unlatched the door under the back stairs and let Marcus go ahead of her.

'I can see why you don't like it down here, it's seriously manky and the light's awful,' he said, peering into one of the wine bays. 'How about we start in here, it really stinks?'

She nodded and went in, her eyes scanning the line of the low arched ceiling, noticed how it curved downwards before disappearing into the dark corners where it joined the flaking whitewashed walls.

'This will do,' she said, perching precariously on a lopsided pile of mouldering newspapers.

'You ready?' he asked.

'Yes, only this isn't very comfortable. Wait while I go and find something nicer to sit on,' she said, and jumping to her feet, dusted herself down. She collected together an armful of cushions and rugs from the playroom and clutching a Christmas candle shaped like an angel, returned to the cellar.

'That's better,' she said, striking a match.

Marcus took one look at the flame coming from the top of the angel's head and snorted, 'It's okay now, but your angel will be headless like your French ancestors before long.'

'*Marcus!*' Tatiana's hands flew to her cheeks as her dream from the night before came flooding back. 'That's reminded me – I think I saw Granny Natasha last night, like she was for real.'

'You kept that very quiet.'

'I'd forgotten till now, like not remembering dreams...'

'Was she a ghost?'

'At the time I thought so. I was so excited at finally seeing her, but then when I woke up I wasn't certain.'

'Did she speak?'

'Sort of, like I could hear her voice, not with my ears, but in my head.'

Marcus nodded. He'd heard about telepathy. 'And is it her in the drawing room?'

'She said not, but guess what? It's so unreal, she told me Isabella's in trouble and I have to rescue her!'

'Rescue Isabella? What'd you mean?' he said looking at her like she'd gone crazy. 'She's been dead for ages!'

'*We* know she's dead, but it seems she doesn't. She's stuck on earth, in France somewhere; has been all these years.'

'A ghost?'

'Yes. So it's simple, all I have to do, is find her ghost, somehow explain to her about being dead and then send her off to heaven!' she said, rolling her eyes.

'Wow! That's some ask.'

'I know, but thinking about it, maybe I do *have* to save her. Maybe all the weird things that keep happening to me, even the peacocks, are somehow connected to her.' As she spoke her stomach lurched, and she wished she'd never remembered her dream.

'Then you have to do it for your own sake, if nothing else,' he said.

'Save *Isabella*?' she whispered. 'How can I possibly save someone who isn't here, who I can't see?'

'You hear things, sense when someone's there.'

'I suppose…' she mumbled. The conversation was making her all jangly like an out-of-tune guitar string, and she didn't like it.

'Now, Tati, back to that stinking place, are you ready?'

'Yes,' she said. 'Only last time it was totally dark so perhaps…'

'You sure,' he asked, raising the flaming angel to his lips.

She nodded, and as the darkness engulfed them, closed her eyes and drew in deep breaths of the foul-smelling air.

Chapter 4

A Physical Link

Tatiana could hear Marcus's breathing and an occasional creak, but otherwise there was complete silence. While waiting and hoping for something to happen, she deliberately slowed her breathing, trying to analyse the sensations caused by the smell. But there were no clues, until a sustained fit of coughing followed by a stifled moan sent her memory spiralling through time. Back two hundred years or more to when she'd been Lisette, the daughter of the Countess Isabella Lafont.

Lisette realised that she must have hit her head because when she came to she was slumped sideways, lying in a crumpled heap on the ground, her senses assaulted by an overpowering stench of sewerage and dead rats. In an attempt not to gag, she pressed her hand over her mouth. *Ye God's! What was this? Her fingers were covered in stinking slime.* She swivelled hastily to her knees, reaching into the darkness, patting the ground around her. *Soggy straw! But what was the sludgy stuff oozing between her fingers?* Unable to stop herself, she retched – she didn't need light to tell her what it was, she could guess – *festering turds!* That must be what she'd slipped on, making her fall. She was struggling to her feet when she felt her ankle seized. She tensed, waiting and fearful of making a sound, until hearing André Imertinsky's familiar voice. 'Are you hurt?' he asked.

'I think not, just mired from … what happened?' she whispered.

'We must have fallen—' he was saying when a prolonged bout of coughing followed by a muffled groan reverberated from the surrounding walls.

'*Hell's teeth, she sounds ill,*' he said.

The fear in his voice made Lisette tremble. *Please God don't let us be too late.* Then as André's strong hands pulled her to her feet and propelled her towards the sound of laboured breathing, her maman's voice rasped the air.

'Cousin André? Is that really you, or do I hallucinate?'

'Indeed it is, Madame, and your daughter too, but my apologies for we're in a most disagreeable state and not fit to be seen, yet I know not how this has come about.'

'Most likely you were pushed and fell. The steps are uneven and treacherous enough to descend even when lit.'

'Why should someone push us?' asked Lisette.

'We are visitors, not prisoners to be treated so roughly,' said André. 'Our identity papers prove that. We've come with food and fresh clothes for you,' he said, reaching out to the huddled figure scratching herself on a pallet of soiled straw. 'At least that is permitted, and candles of course, enough to last until your release can be negotiated.'

While he was talking, Lisette sank to her knees, groping for the bundle.

'I have misplaced the things sent by Henriette,' she said.

'*Non*, they will have been taken, the injuries you sustained when you fell have made you forget what the authorities do here,' came her mother's voice from the darkness.

'I don't recall ... but my head throbs ... and something's crusting my eye,' said André.

'Blood I expect. You should never have risked coming to this place, Monsieur, and certainly not have brought Lisette,' said her maman wearily. Then continuing in a lowered voice, 'Now you both will be sent before the tribunal and condemned, even as I am.'

'Odd's Fish, Madame, I'm a foreigner in this cursed country, nothing to do with the troubles, and your daughter's but a child.'

'Yes, and I too am a foreigner.'

'No longer, having married a royalist. But have faith, I have sworn on my life to get you away from this hell to safety, there is a plan and—' He patted his coat. 'Madame,' he exclaimed, 'we are favoured! They didn't search my pockets! We have candles, a tinderbox…'

'And the cheeses Henriette insisted shouldn't be placed in the bundle with your clean clothes, I have those safe,' said Lisette inching closer to where her mother lay.

Tatiana sat up and blinked. *Who was that stretching?*

'You awake, Tati?'

'Yes. Can you light the candle?' she whispered. As the candle flickered to life Tatiana yawned, rubbed her nose vigorously, and staring blankly at Marcus, blinked. 'It's you?'

'Of course, who did you expect?'

'You… Only I was in this disgusting, stinking prison with … Isabella who *was* my mum back then and someone else. Someone I knew well, whom she called "Cousin André",' she said, and screwing up her eyes, continued to squint absentmindedly at him.

'Who?'

'Difficult to say because it was very dark, even after he'd lit a candle, but I recognised his voice.'

'Well, you sounded really peculiar, as if you were in a costume drama on telly, so who were you?'

'I felt like me, but knew I wasn't because they called me Lisette and I was wearing a dress that trailed on the ground, and the man was in knee-length breeches and a tightly fitting coat with what looked like an uncomfortably high collar,' she said, inspecting her outstretched jean-clad legs.'

'And the smell?'

'The same as here only far, far worse because there obviously wasn't a loo in the cell.'

Leaving the cellars, they sauntered past the kitchen where

Tatiana's mum was baking mince pies and singing along to Christmas music on the radio. 'Yummy smell, Mum, can we have one?' asked Tatiana.

'No, they're still hot,' she said, pushing her hair from her face with a floury hand.

'Oh please, just one,' said Tatiana, and grabbing two, she beat a hasty retreat before her mum could object.

Back in the playroom they ate their pies and continued discussing Tatiana's cellar experience. After a while, she stopped licking her fingers and turned her gaze on Marcus. 'It must have been during the French Revolution, because that fits with Isabella, and have you noticed how these daydreams seem to be connected.'

'I don't think they're dreams exactly,' said Marcus.

'What then?'

'Flashbacks,' he said, 'to a previous life.'

Tatiana's eyes grew ever wider. 'But why?'

'I think they're probably showing you something you *need* to do?' But I'm only guessing.'

Tatiana shivered violently, a sign that told her he was probably right. 'That can only mean one thing – Isabella,' she said with a burst of nervous laughter.

Marcus nodded. 'To the drawing room then?'

It wasn't until after supper that Marcus and Tatiana got the opportunity to start their investigations in the drawing room. The room was dark apart from a welcoming glow from the twinkling of tiny lights decorating the fir tree.

'Ah! It's so pretty and Christmassy in here,' said Tatiana.

'And not the least bit spooky,' said Marcus. 'So when is it?'

'Mostly when I'm playing the piano,' she said.

'Play something then.'

While Tatiana played, Marcus, hands in pockets, wandered slowly around the room.

'Feel anything?' she asked.

'No, but I'm unlikely to ... except I do keep wanting to look over my shoulder.'

'Good, I get that feeling all the time.'

He was looking at the portrait, when he said, 'I know it's probably silly, but should we kowtow to her?

'Yes, just in case,' she said.

They both knelt on the carpet in front of the portrait, raised their arms in the air and in unison, bowed forward, pressing their foreheads to the carpet, their bottoms sticking up in the air, like two ducks foraging on a pond. 'That should placate her ... if it is her,' he said.

While Tatiana went back to playing, Marcus inspected the objects on the mantelpiece; she didn't think there was much to interest him there other than the silver cup containing her grandmother Natasha's ashes, and that *was* interesting. She remembered his expression when he'd first seen it; he'd lifted the lid, and stared at the coarse grey powder, his eyes like saucers. 'Was this really a person?' he'd asked. But, now she could see he was merely curious. His next point of focus was the portrait. She noticed him walking backwards and forwards testing her observation about how the eyes followed you; then he stopped, his attention caught by a movement in the grate. A small curly white feather, caught by an updraught, was spiralling lazily in the air. They exchanged questioning glances, but Tatiana just shook her head and went on playing.

It wasn't until she gave up struggling with a complex piece of Chopin and switched to playing 'her tune' that the atmosphere in the room changed.

She was humming, '*Is anybody there*?' when she saw Marcus stiffen. *So he could feel it too.*

'Keep singing, whatever you do, don't—' he was saying when the Christmas tree lights flickered several times and went off. In the seconds of darkness before they were restored, she heard a sharp intake of breath.

'Now you see what I mean,' she said as a blast of icy air swept through the room.

Tatiana hunched down and continued singing. *'The ghost of Christmases past is definitely here…'*

'Can you see anything?' whispered Marcus. Tatiana shook her head, but she saw him shiver and cross his arms, as pressing his back to the wall, he stared, like a rabbit in the headlights, at the picture.

'What do you want?' he sang. After a few minutes when nothing more had happened, he turned to Tatiana saying, 'Nothing's changing, but then what can? It's not as if Isabella will step out of the frame like in some Harry Potter film or the ashes rise from the urn shaped like a human, that's not possible. But we could do with some tangible evidence whoever you are.'

'I need a trigger,' sang Tatiana.

'You have, it's *your* tune. That's what did it,' Marcus said in a normal voice. Tatiana had stopped playing when a rasping sound coming from the picture caused their breathing to quicken.

'What on earth was that?' she whispered.

'It *is* the picture. Let's get out of here,' he said, leaping for the door.

'No! Wait, we have to see what that is.'

She grabbed Marcus's arm and was pulling him towards the sofa, when the noise stopped, leaving them confronting the picture in a taut silence.

'How about we hum your tune again?'

The moment they started humming, the scratching began again. They remained transfixed, hardly able to sing as something small and grey began to emerge below the lower edge of the heavy gilt frame. They watched, their eyes unwavering, as very slowly, the object slid further and further into view until it became evident that it was nothing more sinister than a piece of paper, suspended from a dusty cobweb.

Tatiana uncrossed her arms and exhaled. 'Mission over!'

'What do you mean?' asked Marcus

'*It's* gone. Haven't you noticed? The rooms warm, and it's delivered a message.'

'How do you know?'

Tatiana shrugged, I don't, but *that* must be something,' she said, jumping to her feet and pointing.

'What is it?'

'I'll look.' Gingerly, she prodded the yellowish-grey paper with a fingertip; she couldn't let Marcus think she was scared of a piece of paper. In one quick movement, she seized it, rubbed the cobwebs off on her jeans, and held it out to Marcus.

'Look! An envelope thingy,' she said. 'And there's something lumpy inside.'

'See what it is, Tati.'

She turned the paper over to reveal the words, 'Isabella 1788'. Underneath someone had added, in now almost illegible brown ink, 'Presented to her daughter, Lisette in 1795'. Tatiana's heart missed a beat. *Her again*. Catching her breath, she turned back the brittle folds to expose a tiny piece of fraying sprigged-muslin containing a lock of sandy-coloured hair bound with blue thread.

'*Bloody hell!* It's *her* hair,' gasped Marcus. 'Now you've got a trigger and a direct link to her. This is an omen, Tati, a warning telling you to do something.'

'Like what?'

'Rescue her of course. It's obvious, *you* have to do it, not only for her, but to rid yourself of … *it*.'

The next day, Marcus and Tatiana agreed that she needed to get back to her French 'maze dream', and see if it could be linked to Isabella since the problems seemed to stem from her.

Hoping not to be interrupted, they closed the shutters and drew the curtains in the playroom, then with paper and pencil at the ready, Marcus waited for Tatiana to settle down and begin. Folding her legs, spider-like under her, she snuggled into an armchair and cupping the lock of hair between her palms, closed her eyes. Her mind whirled with thoughts of Isabella, visualising her as she looked in the picture, then in prison, but that was no good. *Somehow she had to imagine herself back in the maze, even thinking about peacocks might be helpful.* She was still getting nowhere when all thoughts were extinguished by a piercing eeeooowww.

Chapter 5

Revolution – 18th century France

Tatiana didn't speak for ages and Marcus was beginning to think she'd dozed off, when she startled him by punching the air and shouting, '*Vive La France*!'

He waited, pencil poised. 'What's happening, Tati?'

'Il y a beaucoup des persons ici. j'ai peur… '

'In English, Tatiana, I can't understand you.'

'Pardon, Monsieur Imertinsky, mais je suis Lisette. Qui est Tatiana? Je ne connais pas cette fille…'

'*English*,' shouted Marcus.

Tatiana went silent and Marcus was afraid he'd ruined it when she began again, this time in faltering English. He picked up his pencil and started to write.

'The noise, it is terrible; the people outside yell rude words, horrid frightening things and beat the locked gates with weapons.'

'What sort of weapons?' asked Marcus.

'Pitchforks, spades, all sorts of crude farm implements, some women have long kitchen knives, others stout sticks. I think they want food, but others want to kill us and they shout for justice.'

'When is this?'

'The year 1791 of Our Lord,' she said, crossing herself.

'Are you alone?'

'No. We're together.'

'Who's 'we'?' There was a long pause before she answered.

'Granny Natasha's here,' she said in her normal voice. 'I've seen her.'

Tatiana went quiet. Lisette's hand had been seized by Monsieur Imertinsky, her fingers crushed in his vice-like grip as he dragged her unceremoniously away from the baying rabble outside the gates. She stumbled over the hem of her flowing dress and struggled to keep up with his long stride, as they hurtled through a stone arch leading to the terrace at the back of the chateau. Once out of sight of the hostile mob, Monsieur Imertinsky slowed his pace, allowing her to catch her breath.

'Why do they hate us so, Monsieur?' she asked.

'They say they're hungry, but those people weren't from here, Lisette, country people have plenty of food; they were agitators from the town. It's the people in Paris who have no food, but that's been done on purpose by stopping supplies reaching the cities. Hunger's good for stirring up revolutions, people starving, that breeds hate,' he said, more to himself than to her.

'Why us?'

'You live in a chateau. You're an aristocrat, privileged, that's why.'

Lisette's mind was spinning like one of her brother's tops as they continued silently along the paved terrace. She glanced wistfully at a flight of elegantly curving steps, hoping André might allow her to escape to the gardens below. She longed to run away and hide amongst the neatly trimmed hedges of the parterre and cleanse the ugly, threatening voices of the crowd from her mind with the gentle sounds of the cascading fountains. Just the thought of being trapped inside the chateau and unable to get out made her guts churn.

'Come, I have to take you to your mother, she's anxious to see you.'

'Maman here? I thought she was at Versailles with Papa and Cécile.'

'No. She has been a little unwell and with all the unrest in Paris your father, *le Comte,* ordered her home until she is fully recovered; she arrived shortly before the gates were closed against the mob.'

With André Imertinsky still holding firmly onto her hand,

they entered the chateau by a side door, ran up the wide staircase to the first floor and along the dazzling gallery where the gilded mirrors reflected the sunlight streaming through the windows opposite.

'Go to your maman now,' he said, giving her a gentle push. 'She's waiting for you in the green salon.'

Lisette ran along the polished floor, allowing her feet to slide when she thought none of the hovering servants were watching. She liked to *glisser,* just like sliding on ice in the winter, only it wasn't permitted; it wasn't ladylike and Mademoiselle Palazot would scold her if she saw. She did a final slide to a halt outside her mother's apartments, paused to straighten her dress and smooth her hair, and then knocked.

'*Entrez,*' came from within.

Lisette leant against the heavy door, entered, and with her head down crossed the room, passing her mother's attendants with barely a nod of recognition, to the far end where her mother was supervising the unpacking of her jewels.

'Not those, these, I will wear them tonight. *Oui, naturellement, les émeraudes,*' she said, glaring at her maid.

'Maman.'

'Lisette, mon petit chou, comment va-tu?'

'Well, I thank you, Madame,' she said, bobbing a curtsey. 'And you, Maman, how are you … and Papa? Is he not here?'

'He is well, child, but with the problems in Paris he could not come. I also am well enough, just a trifling cough, but he would insist on my coming to the country for some fresh air, so annoying of him,' she said, pursing her lips.

'And Cécile, did she come with you?' she asked, trying not to sound too excited.

'No, she remains at court, unlike me, your father wanted her to stay with him and her aunt despite the so called "disturbances".'

Lisette's face fell. She didn't mind her scary father not

returning to the country, but she'd been totally bereft since her dearest friend and companion had been sent away, to live at Versailles and make a suitable marriage.

'I wish she had come home too, it's so very dull without her.'

'You seem to forget your half-sister is much older than you. When you're sixteen, you shall go to court too.'

'But I have no one to play with, to share my secrets … it's – it's like *half* of me is missing without her,' she said, sighing.

'It's no good looking so mournful, besides, you still have Jean-Louis,' her maman said, turning abruptly away, but not before Lisette noticed her usually serene face had taken on a pinched look, making her think that maybe she didn't care for Cécile very much. Yes. Her maman was right; she did have her mischievous little brother for company – that was when he wasn't ill in bed, which he frequently was.

Lisette perched on the edge of an open trunk and watched her mother as she moved about the room with light steps. She admired her delicate beauty, her porcelain white skin and slender figure, She gazed at her mother's beautiful clothes lying in the unpacked trunk and fingered the fine silks and exquisite embroidery pressing the soft damasks and velvets to her cheek and running the long satin ribbons through her fingers: they smelt of her, a scent that made her feel safe. But were they safe? Just the thinking of what she'd seen made her heart pound. But her maman didn't seem concerned by what was happening beyond the chateau walls, so maybe she shouldn't worry either.

She hoped to be allowed to stay with her maman and hear stories about life at court, her father, his handsome new secretary, the Chevalier Pellerin and above all, her beloved Cécile. She longed to know how Cécile filled her days and if she had fallen in love with any of her suitors. She hoped not, especially not Henri Pellerin, she couldn't bear that. Cécile could marry anyone other than him. But her maman was too occupied with other things and it wasn't long before she signalled to one of the ladies to take her away. She smiled as Henriette Palazot came towards her, for she knew her well. It was Henriette who arranged her tuition, dancing lessons, engaged her music teachers and even instructed her in the arts of embroidery, drawing and painting. She ordered the making of Lisette's clothes, chose the cloth and instructed her personal maid how to dress her hair; and unlike her mother – the beautiful Countess Isabella – who was frequently with the court at Versailles, Henriette was always at Clèrmency with her and Jean-Louis.

Having paid her respects to her maman, she was then allowed outside to amuse herself in the gardens, so long as she stayed well away from the main gates. Mademoiselle Henriette placed a blue velvet cloak over her dress, tying it at the neck with wide ribbons before accompanying Lisette to the terrace. As they walked in the sun Lisette bombarded Henriette with questions about what was happening in the world beyond the chateau walls to make the village people so angry with them. Henriette told her about the menacing fear creeping like a cancer over France, spreading out from the cities and infecting the once quiet and peaceful countryside, bringing doubt and fear into the hearts of the ordinary citizens of France.

She was still talking when the discordant sound of instruments being tuned drifted from the open windows of the grand salon. They stopped and looking through the window saw Monsieur Imertinsky, her mother's musically talented cousin, talking to the assembled musicians. Lisette knew he'd arrange something special for her maman that night to celebrate her return home, for she'd often observed how anxious he was to please her. Before long their downcast spirits were cast aside as the air filled with a pulsating harmony, music so heavenly it could only come from the beating of angelic wings.

'Ah, *c'est La Reine,'* Henriette said, sighing.

'I know this, it's my song.'

'Not *your* song, Lisette, Haydn's. It's quite the Queen's

favourite and frequently played at court.'

Lisette, noticing that Henriette had never once taken her eyes off André Imertinsky's strong, good-looking face, and was evidently not only captivated by the music, but also by him, seized the opportunity to make her escape. She raised the hem of her skirt and with her blue cloak billowing behind, tripped sedately down the broad steps to the formal gardens below, but once out of sight, she hoisted her skirts higher and ran as fast as she could towards the distant maze. She was nearing the entrance when, rounding a corner she nearly collided with a pair of white peacocks strutting across the path. Her shoes skidded to a halt on the gravel. The birds looked expectantly at her. 'Bother!' She hadn't brought anything for them, and she could see they were hoping for a treat. She was debating whether to go back for some bread, when she became aware of a mounting roar amidst the babble of voices coming from behind the chateau. As the sound rose to a crescendo she heard a high-pitched, blood-curdling scream. A wave of foreboding tightened in her stomach as she sensed something terrible was about to happen. A moment later she heard Henriette calling, her words obscured by the shrieking of the peacocks.

Tatiana sat up, opened her mouth and screamed.

'*Tati! What's the matter*?' asked Marcus, clamping his hands to his ears.

'You know.'

'No I don't, you've been silent for ages,' said Marcus. 'I thought you'd gone to sleep.'

'*Asleep!* No way! Not there.'

'Tell me what happened. I need to fill in the gaps.'

'Marcus,' she said, grasping his arm, 'it was like watching a film, and really awesome, because I was there, in it.'

'No you weren't, you were *really* here,' said Marcus.

'But I was … well my mind was; and now I understand about

the peacocks and why Isabella looks so sad, and guess what? You were there too!'

'Was I? When I've been here, awake all the time.'

'Yes, but a different you.'

'How do you know?'

'Well you didn't look like you, but then I didn't look much like me; this me that is, because she was me too, you see?'

'No. I don't see. Slow down and explain, Tati.'

'I knew that Lisette was me, that I was her, and other people, like you, I recognised, not by how you looked but by – by how you felt … like seeing two people at once, it was really brilliant.'

Marcus blinked and shook his head. 'Did the others realise about you?'

'Of course not, because I was *remembering* that lifetime, not living it. I have the feeling that only the now us can "see" the before "them", but the "them" that are—'

'Tati! You're talking gobbledygook.'

'I'm not. Well maybe, because now I think about it, it is a bit confusing, although it made perfect sense to me at the time. Shall I begin again?'

'No! Please don't. But write everything down before you forget, then we'll compare notes.'

Tatiana's pencil flew across the paper. 'You see, Marcus, my maze dream wasn't a just a dream, but a fragment of memory, because just now, when I was Lisette, I was wearing a blue velvet cloak, like the girl in my dream.'

'Then who were you in the dream?'

'I was me, Tatiana seeing, or rather dreaming about an episode from an earlier life when I was Lisette and all because of the peacock,' said Tatiana. *Did that make sense? Could she really have been Lisette or was it just wishful thinking?*

'I see,' said Marcus scratching his head. 'You associate peacocks with the French Revolution, so every time you hear them, it reminds some part of you of the horrors and scares you.'

'Something like that, only I wasn't aware of it until now.'

'But it must have already been inside you for you to remember it.'

Now it was Tatiana's turn to look puzzled, and not understanding how she could remember something that hadn't happened to her personally, ignored Marcus's observation.

'So in a previous life Isabella *was* my mother.'

'And you're sure you saw me?'

'Yes, I told you.'

'So who was I?' asked Marcus.

'I'm not going to say. Not yet. Not till I'm absolutely certain.' Tatiana said, fixing Marcus with a penetrating look.

Tatiana hummed as she later pottered around her room getting ready for bed. In the back of a drawer she'd found a small leather jewel box her mum had given her, lined it with tissue to keep Isabella's hair safe, then tucked it under her pillow.

'Now, for some really good dreams', she murmured, climbing into bed. But first, where was Pushkin? She always slept with her, so she must have got shut in somewhere. Tatiana slipped out of bed and padded downstairs. First she checked Pushkin's basket in the kitchen, then the playroom. She wondered if she'd gone out mousing, or, *'Oh no!'* Far more likely, she'd got shut in the drawing room. Gritting her teeth, she faced the closed door; there was nothing for it, she had to go in.

She took a deep breath, grabbed the door handle and pushed. The room was in darkness and the light switch out of reach. Not wanting to brave the darkened room, she called from the doorway, *'Pushkin?'* With no answering meow she was closing the door when she sensed something stir within.

'Pushkin?' She nudged the door with her foot allowing the passage light to penetrate further inside; then she saw her, crouched on the back of the sofa, fur standing on end, staring at the wall opposite.

With one bound she was beside her. 'What *are* you doing?' she asked smoothing her coat. She was about to pick her up, when she saw what Pushkin was looking at. For a moment she couldn't move, her outstretched hands remained frozen mid-movement as she registered with absolute clarity a pair of disembodied eyes. No face, no hair or body, nothing but pale blue eyes – looking straight at her. With her own eyes growing ever rounder, she watched as more of the face gradually emerged until she could make out a small button nose floating inches from her own. Too startled to scream, she remained rigid as a mouth appeared; then just when she couldn't bear it any longer, the lips parted in a wide grin exposing a gummy gap where the two front teeth should have been. As her hands flew to cover her mouth, the face dissolved, swallowed by the darkness.

'*Who are you*?' she asked in a hoarse whisper. But the face had gone and before anything else could appear, she seized Pushkin and ignoring the small white feather being blown towards her, bolted from the room.

Back in the safety of her bedroom she collapsed onto her bed hugging Pushkin. 'I so wanted to see what '*it*' was, but now I really wish I hadn't!' she told her struggling cat. After a few minutes she released Pushkin; *should she tell Marcus, or wait till morning?* Perhaps she'd wait, give herself time to rationalize her thoughts and decide exactly what it was she'd seen. For weeks she'd been hoping to see something, anything, and now something so bizarre and beyond her wildest imaginings had materialised when least expected. Yes, it had scared and excited her, in equal measure; that had been something 'other', a ghost, and there was no doubt this time, she was awake.

Chapter 6

An Invitation

The following day, while waiting for his mum to arrive, Marcus and Tatiana returned to the playroom where she told him about the eyes in the drawing room.

'It sounds like the grinning cat from *Alice in Wonderland*,' said Marcus. 'But why no teeth?'

Tatiana frowned. 'He looked about six or seven so they might have fallen out.'

Marcus was shaking his head when, for a second, his face clouded. 'You said it was *smiling*, so it was friendly then. Are you sure it wasn't baring its teeth?'

Tatiana wrapped her arms tighter around herself. 'You mean snarling? Like threatening me?'

'Don't know, just a thought. And you keep saying "he" like it was a boy,' he said, scrutinizing her worried expression.

'Do I?'

Marcus nodded. 'But hey, a boy's better than a cat! You've been gagging to see a ghost, and now you have!'

'I know,' she said, wrinkling her nose. 'But not that one. I wanted to see granny.'

'I don't think you get to choose with ghosts,' said Marcus. 'Anyway, now you've seen something, maybe you should try again.'

Tatiana pulled a face. 'In the drawing room?'

'Yes. And don't look so worried, I'll be with you.'

The wintery sun was low in the sky and long shadows slanting through the drawing room's low-leaded windows made jagged patterns on the Turkish rug by the fireplace. Tatiana wanted to put the tree lights on and eliminate the shadowy uncertainty from the room, but Marcus wouldn't let her, saying it would spoil the atmosphere.

'I suppose I'd better sit here,' she said, perching on the edge of the sofa. 'This is where I saw it last night.'

Tatiana sat down and reluctant to close her eyes, focused her attention on Isabella's impassive face. She didn't really fancy trying to summon up the body-less-one again, but then, she supposed she'd have to. For a while nothing happened; then a series of disjointed images flashed into her mind. The first was of a woman, alone in a large airy room. She was dancing with a small dog cradled in her arms, when there was an explosion of splintering wood as a door burst open. Then she saw soldiers in blue and white uniforms carrying muskets topped by glistening steel bayonets, their faces grim and determined as they forced their way through a sullen crowd. The last was of a child with long curly corn-coloured hair wearing an embroidered waistcoat and sky-blue breeches.

'Was it a boy?' exclaimed Marcus, after she described what she'd seen.

'I don't know, it looked more like a girl in fancy dress to me than 'it' from last night.'

'Pity he didn't smile.'

Grimacing, Tatiana went on, 'The soldiers felt hostile, as if they were after me, and, like a nightmare, I knew no matter what, I couldn't escape them. The woman with the dog, although of the same time and obviously in danger, was different.'

'In what way?'

'She was a bit creepy with her white face-paint and birds nest of a wig, and either she was unaware or simply indifferent to any impending danger, but then maybe I felt the danger and she didn't – so just a useless muddle.'

'Maybe not, for a start, the woman might have been Isabella, and the child could also be connected. But why the crowd of people and soldiers?' murmured Marcus.

Tatiana shook her head. 'I don't know. They were only flashes, no one spoke and nothing actually happened except for the soldiers coming for me ... but they, unlike the crowd, were clean with smart uniforms and funky three-sided black hats with rosette thingy's stuck on the side. There was something ominous about the rosettes though, because when I saw them, shivers shot right through me.

'Those were tricorne hats with cockades pinned on them. What colour were they, Tatiana?'

'Red, white and blue, like a bull's-eye, I think. Why so excited by a hat?' she asked.

'Because at last it's beginning to make sense. Those were soldiers of the National Guard, the French Revolutionary Army! Don't you see, everything you've seen *is* connected to Isabella!'

Tatiana nodded and looking around the room said, 'Except the toothless one and I know he won't leave me alone until I've rescued Isabella, and that's *so* impossible ... unless...'

'You can do it, Tati.'

'*Really?* How do you rescue a ghost exactly?'

'Not a clue. What about Googling it?'

'Marcus, granny said *you'd* help!'

He shrugged. 'How can I when she's somewhere in France? You'll have to try at Christmas when you're staying with your grandfather in Paris, which means without me.'

Tatiana bit her lower lip. Outwardly she was trying hard to appear normal, but icy tentacles were pressing in on her insides making it difficult to breath. She knew she had to do it, only was completely flummoxed as to how to achieve something so obscure. For one thing she didn't know how, and for another, her mum would never let her go wandering off on her own in Paris shouting, '*Is anybody there*?' She was still wondering how to enlist Marcus's help, when her mum calling interrupted all thoughts.

'Marcus! Your mum's here.'

Marcus was enveloped in a goodbye embrace from his aunt Katya when Tatiana caught his eye. *He was grinning! How dare he?* There he was happily going home for Christmas leaving her with the unresolved issues of *'it'* and Isabella. She could feel the blood draining from her face, but she refused to panic. Instead she took a deep breath and clenching her fists behind her back, resolved not to be defeated, there wasn't time — she had to do something, and now.

'What's the matter, darling, you don't look at all well?'

Ignoring her mum, Tatiana turned to her aunt. 'Aunt Sally, can Marcus come for Christmas?' She was aware of Marcus beside her pulling a 'what the hell face?' and a surprised look on her mum's, but she didn't care. '*Please* say he can.'

'Er ... that's very kind of you,' his mum said, looking quizzically at Katya. 'But won't you be in France?'

'Yes, can he come too?'

'Well, it's really up to Marcus ... if he wants—'

Before he had a chance to answer, Tatiana's mum, warming to the idea, joined in. 'Do come with us, Marcus, poor Tati gets awfully bored staying with her grandfather. If you came, then you could explore Paris together.'

Marcus's eyebrows shot up as he and Tatiana exchanged glances.

'Marcus hasn't been away at Christmas before,' said his mum.

'How about joining us afterwards then?' her mum said. 'What do you say Marcus?'

Marcus ran both hands through his hair making his usually floppy fringe stand on end. 'Well, um, I've never been to Paris.'

'*Oh do let him come*, Aunt Sally,' Tatiana pleaded. Her head was suddenly buzzing with ideas of how she'd get Marcus to help her find Isabella; he just had to come, because once there, he'd have no choice, but to help her.

'Well, if you really mean it, Marcus.'

'Brilliant! That's just awesome,' Marcus said, a broad grin

spreading across his face. 'Can I fly?'

'Take the train under the channel, the Eurostar's really the best,' said Tatiana, skipping as she followed Marcus out to the car.

Hugging Marcus tight, she whispered, 'It's really fantastic you coming. Grand-père's really old and since Granny Natasha died he doesn't go out much and Mum spends all her time with him so it's usually dead boring.'

'Don't you go out?'

'Yes, of course, but Mum never lets me go off on my own.'

'But she will if you're with me, she's just said so.'

'She'd better,' Tatiana said, grinning for the first time in days. 'And don't worry about Grand-père, he may be old and doddery, but he's a character and tells wonderful stories.'

His mum was driving off when Marcus stuck his head out of the window. 'See you in Paris, Tati.'

'Yes! And we're on a rescue mission remember,' yelled Tatiana, waving at the departing car.

'A rescue mission, what's that about?' asked her mum.

Tatiana shrugged and said, 'Nothing, nothing at all.'

Chapter 7

Drawing a Blank

Tatiana saw from the overhead information screens at the Gare du Nord that Marcus's train from London had arrived on time, only she could see no sign of him amongst the mass of humanity spilling onto the concourse. She was beginning to think he'd missed the train when she spotted him, inspecting his nails, obviously trying his best to look cool and nonchalant, like he travelled to Paris every day of the week.

'Marcus! Over here!' she shouted, jumping up and down waving.

'Phew! Tati, I thought you weren't here,' he said, as an unstoppable grin spread across his face.

'This is so exciting!'

'How was the journey, darling?' asked his aunt, planting lipsticky kisses on both his cheeks.

'Really great, and you'll never believe it, the Eurostar was quicker than the train from home to London!' he said, freeing himself from his aunt's enveloping embrace.

'Bring your rucksack and let's go,' said Tatiana, propelling Marcus towards the exit.

As soon as they reached the family apartment in the Marais, Tatiana took Marcus to meet her grandfather, Grand-père Jacques. He'd been snoozing in a chair by the fire, and was struggling to his feet blinking owlishly as they came in. Scowling, he flicked at wisps of grey hair hanging over his eyes before thrusting a bony hand at Marcus. His strong face, once handsome, was now craggy and deeply furrowed from a long life well lived. Marcus immediately liked the look of him and after a few minutes together it became apparent they were going to get along. A smile flashed across Tatiana's face. She'd not wanted to put Marcus off coming so hadn't warned him that her grandfather had become rather grumpy and intolerant in his old age, particularly with people he didn't know. Tatiana looked at the two of them now, their heads bent together, poring over the book Marcus had given her grandfather as a thank-you present for having him to stay.

'This is an exceptional gift, young man,' Tatiana's grandfather said, turning the book over and over in his sinewy hands. 'It's rare to find such a fine copy, *and* translated into English I see.'

'It's about the Revolution,' Marcus said.

'Indeed it is, and are you interested in French history?'

'Yes. Well, only because of the picture of Isabella at Tati's home.'

'Ah yes, *that* picture. It used to hang here you know.'

'Oh! Of course,' said Marcus.

'It belonged to my dear wife, Natasha, and she left it to Tati's mother when she died. Katya wanted it to stay here until I shuffle off, but I insisted on her taking it, didn't want it around causing any more trouble, besides we don't want any muddle with those tax men when I'm dead, do we?'

Marcus wasn't too sure what taxmen had to do with dead people's pictures, but as his mind was racing, he just nodded absentmindedly.

'We want to find out about her ... she looks so sad.'

For a moment Jacques eyes narrowed. 'Just what Natasha used to say. She became *obsessed* by that woman and it wasn't healthy,' he said, rounding on Marcus wagging his finger as if it was his fault. 'If you take my advice, young man, you'll forget about her and not go disturbing the dead.'

Tatiana showed Marcus to a narrow room with fabric-covered walls and tall, shuttered windows. 'This is where you're sleeping,' she said, and opening the windows, folded back the louvered shutters so Marcus could see the Christmas lights decorating the bay trees in the courtyard below and hear the cry of the chestnut seller in the street beyond.

'Wow! Tati, this is … brilliant!'

She grinned. 'Yes, very chic, and very French.'

The apartment occupied half of the first floor of what had once been a grand house built around a central courtyard. The salon with its three, heavily-draped widows, high ceiling and large fireplace had an air of decaying grandeur, not helped by a large expanse of un-faded wallpaper where the portrait had hung. The furniture was old-fashioned; the formal chairs stiffly upholstered and uncomfortable, and every available surface covered in layers of clutter. Tatiana took Marcus into the kitchen where the smells of Christmassy pine and cigarette smoke, present throughout the apartment, were replaced by a tantalising smell of mushrooms being cooked with garlic and thyme.

'You must be hungry,' said Tatiana, as Marcus's stomach emitted a loud rumble.

The next morning her mum made a list of places for Marcus to see. She had a street map of Paris opened out on the breakfast table, a guidebook in English, a plan of the Metro and a list of instructions for Tatiana.

'I'm taking father to visit a friend today, so I thought you could start by going up the Eiffel Tower, then take a bateau-mouche to the Louvre where you can show Marcus the Mona Lisa; then after lunch in a café you can walk across to the Île-de-la-Cité, followed by—'

'*Mum*!'

'What's the matter, will it be too much?'

'No, it's just that with only eight days *to do everything*,' she said, looking pointedly at Marcus, 'we've other plans.'

'Like what?'

'We thought we'd go to the Concièrgerie. I want to show him

where Marie Antoinette was imprisoned before losing her head.'

'And the Place de la Concorde where the executions took place,' added Marcus.

'I'm afraid you'll find Concorde a bit disappointing. The square is just a huge traffic-jam these days. Couldn't you go somewhere more cheerful?' said her mum.

'We will once we've found out what happened to Isabella,' said Tatiana. 'What we need is to find prison records and lists of everyone executed during the Revolution.'

Her mum frowned. 'Goodness! I don't know where you'll find those; literally thousands of people were guillotined all over the country. And as for Isabella, she was such a minor aristocrat I don't suppose there'll be any mention of her.'

Since they really had no idea how to find the ghost of some long-dead person, who mightn't even have died in Paris, Marcus and Tatiana decided to start by visiting some of the places connected to the Revolution.

They wound their way along cobbled streets, lingered by small cafés breathing in the warm scents of freshly baked bread drifting from the basement kitchens and pressed their noses against patisserie windows to marvel at the pyramids of brightly coloured macaroons and displays of pastries, the like of which Marcus had never seen. They continued on to the main shopping area, busy with post-Christmas bargain hunters, stopping occasionally to window shop or for Tatiana to point out places of interest, until they found themselves approaching one of the many bridges crossing the Seine.

'There it is,' said Tatiana, pointing to an imposing turreted building on the opposite bank of the river. 'That's where we're going.'

They entered the *Concièrgerie* through a gloomy stone chamber, which led into a huge and spectacular multi-columned hall. They proceeded through room after room, one containing relics of the Revolution including a blackened guillotine blade, prison rules and regulations. They saw the cell where Marie-Antoinette spent her final days and pored over lists of prisoners; reading about their torture and eventual deaths, but nowhere was there any reference to Isabella.

'Your mum was right.'

'Yes, but there're meant to be *loads of ghosts* in this place,' she said, fingering the small box in her pocket.

'That's all very well, but we can hardly go around shouting, "Is there anybody there?" like that old poem you keep singing, can we?'

'Who says?' said Tatiana, giggling. 'I'll give it a go if you like.'

'*Don't even think about it, Tati*!'

Back in the biting December wind outside, they dithered over where to go next.

'She must have been buried, so shouldn't we look for her grave?' said Tatiana.

'Do you really think ghosts haunt graveyards?'

'No, but if we found her gravestone it might tell us when and where she died,' said Tatiana, thrusting her hands into the warmth of her pockets.

'Ah! A starting point.'

'Exactly.'

'With all the thousands of people killed in the Revolution, there must be a *huge* graveyard somewhere.'

'I know!' cried Tatiana. 'There's a really massive one, Père Lachaise, you'll just love it!'

With Tatiana leading the way they headed towards the nearest Metro station, taking a short cut across the île-de-la-Cité, so Marcus could see the bird market. Passing through a heady scent of lilies and narcissi from stalls stacked high with a kaleidoscope of flowers, they came to the caged birds, where, surrounded by a murmur of soft chirruping, they stopped to admire a lonely Mynah bird. Walking on, they crossed the river and were approaching the Metro when Marcus, side-tracked by a shriek of laughter from a group of students drinking coffee outside a café, nearly ran into a dog doing its business in the middle of the pavement.

'Watch out!' she called.

'That was a near one —' he was saying, when Tatiana nudged him.

'It's not only the dogs,' she said, pointing to a line of pee snaking across the pavement from where a tramp was relieving himself against a wall.

After a short Metro ride they arrived at the cemetery. Once inside the gates they wandered along the straight, tree-lined paths admiring the tombs, which varied enormously in size and style; simple headstones stood alongside replicas of Greek temples; stone crosses beside Egyptian pyramids; grandly carved porticoes over tombs; doors leading to underground crypts; and, everywhere, angels in all shapes, forms and guises. They spotted the names of famous poets, actresses and politicians.

'Look! Oscar Wilde's buried here.'

'And my heroes, Chopin *and* Jim Morrison!'

They darted from stone angel to marble obelisk, eagerly reading the inscriptions until after several hours of fruitless searching Marcus finally blurted out, 'This can't be the right cemetery, Tati.'

'Why not?'

'All the dates I've seen are later than the Revolution!'

'Are you sure?'

'Yes, look, they're all in the 1800s, the Revolution was over by then.'

'We must be in the wrong section,' she said.

'So, let's keep walking. You check the dates on one side while I check the other.'

After another half-hour of wandering up and down the paths

Marcus stopped, and throwing himself down on a gravestone, announced, 'It's no good, the dates are just becoming more recent.'

Tatiana sank down beside him and resting her head in her hands, groaned, 'Just when I really thought we were onto something.' But all the same she couldn't help being secretly relieved, the cemetery was so enormous she'd envisaged spending the entire holidays there.

Later that evening, they were sitting around the fire with Grand-père Jacques, trying hard to be patient as he sifted through a brown leather suitcase crammed full of Natasha's old family papers, when he got up and insisted, despite fierce protestations from her mum, on pouring them all a glass of wine.

'Young people should be taught about wine, learn to respect a fine vintage.'

'But they're too young, Papa,' her mum said, placing a restraining hand on his arm as he poured the crimson liquid into their glasses.

'You had the occasional glass at their age,' he said, winking at Marcus and Tatiana. 'Didn't do you any harm. Anyway it will stop them experimenting behind, how do you call it, the bicycle shed?'

Marcus took a great gulp. 'Sip it!' ordered Tatiana's mum, throwing her father an exasperated look.

Marcus and Tatiana exchanged glances and tried not to giggle as her grandfather went on extolling the virtues of the wine.

'But now for some family history,' he said, settling back in his chair. 'This,' he said, drumming his fingers on the battered cover of a black leather bible, 'is where the Lafont's kept records of births, marriages and deaths, *and* it mentions the woman you're so interested in.' He pushed his glasses up on his nose and started to read. 'Isabella Lafont, formally, Imertinsky born in Russia in 1764. Married Count Philippe Lafont in Paris, August 1783. She was his second wife, his first having died giving birth to a daughter, Cécile, born in 1772. He was a diplomat with the court of Louis XVI at Versailles. They had a son Jean-Louis born, 1782, died 1788, a daughter Lisette...' At the mention of Lisette, Marcus and Tatiana turned towards each other, but neither said a word.

'...born 1776.' He paused.

'And?'

'That's it. Be grateful there's anything at all,' he snapped.

Undaunted by the irritated edge to his voice, Tatiana persisted. 'But when did they die?'

'It doesn't say. Who do you think was left to write such things in the midst of all the turmoil? You're just like your grandmother, obsessed; she *had* to know, and in my opinion, that's what made her ill. Take care Isabella doesn't make you ill too,' he said, scowling at her over the top of his spectacles. The veiled threat made Tatiana clutch her stomach, but she too had to know.

'What did Granny want to know?'

'Like you, she wanted to know about Isabella. She was forever going off to the chateau where she'd lived, doing research she said.'

'Chateau? What did she discover?'

'She didn't tell me. She knew I didn't approve of her sneaking off there like a tourist on open days, when rightfully the place should have belonged to her.'

'So there's no way of knowing what she found out?' she asked.

'Not unless it's in her notebooks.'

'*Notebooks*?'

'Yes. She jotted things down. Anything that amused her, phrases she wanted to remember – never went anywhere without a notebook in her handbag.'

Marcus and Tatiana exchanged excited glances. 'Do you think we could see them?'

Her grandfather scowled and, without answering, lit a cigarette, filling the room with the pungent smell of Gauloises. Tatiana held her breath as he got unsteadily to his feet and shuffled out of the room. 'I'll see if I can find them,' he said.

'Mum, *please* can we go to the chateau?'

'No. Quite out of the question, your grandfather will never allow it.'

'But Isabella lived there – we *have* to go.'

'Nonsense, you don't *have to*, I've never even been myself!'

Her mum sounded terse, but Tatiana, refused to be put off. 'Aren't you interested in our family history, Mum?'

'Of course. I've told you about how the picture got here and all that, haven't I?' she said in a huffy voice.

'Yes, but ages ago, remind me.'

'Well, we know it was painted by Thomas Gainsborough before Isabella's marriage to Lafont, and so must have hung at the family chateau. Many years later it was found, along with other family things, in the Imertinsky house in St Petersburg. That was before the Revolution.'

'*Before* the Revolution?' queried Marcus.

'Not the French one; the Russian Revolution, over a hundred years later. When that started, my great, great grandmother was a small child, and her parents, fearing for their lives, fled Russia and came to Paris. They could only take what would fit in the car with them, but the picture was very valuable so they tied it to the roof! I believe the intention was to sell it as they had little money, but luckily they didn't have to.'

'What was Lafont's stuff doing in Russia?' asked Marcus.

'It was probably taken there at the time Lisette escaped with her governess.'

'So, Granny was right,' murmured Tatiana.

'Backwards and forwards from one Revolution to another,' Marcus was muttering, when Tatiana's grandfather returned carrying a small cardboard box.

'These should keep you quiet,' he said, raising one sardonic eyebrow at Tatiana.

Marcus and Tatiana sat on the floor with the box between them. Inside was a collection of pocket-size notebooks; some spiral bound with 60s multi-coloured covers, others in plain black moleskin. After a brief flick through the collection, Tatiana placed three on the rug and rolling her eyes at Marcus, muttered, 'These are the latest, Marcus, but wait for it—'

'You don't need to tell me – they're in French.'

'Not only that, they're written in a sort of shorthand, and talk about spidery writing! They're going to take *ages* to decipher.'

'It could be worse, they might have been in Russian then we'd really be stuck.'

He was flipping through one of the books when he came across a list. At first the words meant nothing to him, until unexpectedly, a name he recognised leapt up at him. Passing the book to Tatiana, he whispered, 'Look at that.'

As Tatiana scanned the list, her chest filled with a quivering sensation. '*This* is just brilliant, Marcus,' she whispered. She then continued reading, pointing out other names to him, names familiar to them from her dreams.

'Granny mentions someone called Henriette. Was she a relation?' Tatiana asked her grandfather.

'No, but she married one; a Russian fellow called André Imertinsky, a distant cousin of Isabella's, if I remember rightly. It was stories from Henriette's diaries that so intrigued your grandmother.'

'*Diaries*? Is Isabella mentioned in them?'

'I expect so...'

Tatiana elbowed Marcus in the ribs. 'Can we see them?'

'That's not possible; the diaries were left behind in St Petersburg. Natasha was told the stories by her mother. She would undoubtedly have remembered more, but I'm afraid I don't.'

Tatiana turned to her mum. '*Mum*?'

'I should remember,' she said. 'My mother told me so many, many stories, but it was when I was a child and—'

Tatiana threw her mum a look of exasperation. 'Surely someone knows what happened to Isabella, where she died. Grand-père, don't you know?'

'No, child, I've told you, I don't, but Natasha did mention a convent...'

'What convent?'

'I have an idea she was cared for by the nuns at Carmes.'

Tatiana stared at her grandfather. She'd just seen that name in a notebook; maybe it was all in there somewhere – if only granny hadn't been so cryptic.

'Why this fixation with where she died?' asked her mum.

Tatiana, aware that her mum was looking at her very intensely, was wondering what to say, when Marcus, obviously not thinking, blurted out, 'We've made it our mission to find her.'

Tatiana cringed. *How could Marcus say something like that?* Dismayed, she waited for the inevitable sarcastic response from her grandfather, but to her surprise, it didn't come.

'Did you say find *her*?'

'Well ... maybe her ghost ... or something like that,' mumbled Marcus, catching Tatiana's eye. 'You see it says there're loads of them at the Conciègerie.'

'And we thought it would be nice to find Isabella's ghost and...' She started giggling nervously. 'Um ... say some prayers for her or something – don't you think?' said Tatiana, looking apprehensively at her mum.

'*Non*!' retorted her grandfather 'You cannot be so gullible. They just say that to bring in the tourists.'

'But, Grand-père, *you* believe in spirits don't you?'

'*Absolument pas!* Unlike your grandmother, I do not.'

'What about you, Mum?'

'I'm not sure, never having seen one.'

'What if you saw Granny?'

'Stop it. That's quite enough, Tatiana.'

Marcus glanced at Tatiana, who, determined not to be defeated, shrugged mouthing, 'We'll show them.' They hadn't much to go on, but at least they had the notebooks, even if they were practicably illegible; and better still, they had confirmation of people from her 'dreams,' which proved conclusively they were real and not, as she'd feared, figments of her imagination.

'You should try contacting your grandmother,' whispered Marcus. 'She *must* know where Isabella is.'

Tatiana nodded. 'But how? She only appears when *she* wants to.'

'Except this apartment was her home, so she might come visiting your grandfather and Mum, not that they'd be too receptive.'

Or me, thought Tatiana crossing her fingers. *She should visit me. After all this is her unfinished business, not mine.*

Chapter 8

Another Reality

Tatiana was sleeping soundly until disturbed by an icy draught around her neck. She groped for the duvet; *where was it? This was ridiculous; it wasn't on the bed!* But then she discovered, neither was she! She was back in the salon where they'd been sitting after supper; only the room had changed from how it'd been earlier in the evening. The furniture was arranged differently; there were vases of spring flowers where Christmas decorations had been, and in the grate where the fire had blazed so recently, stood a potted plant. Tatiana, realising she must be asleep and that this was a dream, went to turn over in bed only to find herself coming face to face with her grandmother.

Granny!'

'Tatiana, I'm so glad you've come. I need to talk to you.'

'Me too, because—' Tatiana stopped abruptly, staring at the wall behind her grandmother.

'Yes, it's here!' she said, laughing.

'How can it be? It's in the drawing room at home – in England!' she burst out, gesticulating at the portrait of Isabella hanging on the wall in front of them.

'For me the apartment is still how I knew it.'

Tatiana's eyes flew around the room, 'Not … not as it is … now?' she said, her voice trailing away.

'No. When you're dead, the places you knew on earth remain exactly the same, which is why people talk about seeing ghosts disappearing through walls and you, in your sleep state, are seeing it as I do.'

Tatiana tried to gather her thoughts. She urgently needed to quiz her grandmother about Isabella before she disappeared, but was too puzzled to concentrate.

'Granny, this is all very strange, I know that picture is at home … and I know my body is asleep in bed, yet here am I talking to you right in front of it.' Or was she? *Surely this couldn't be happening, she must be dreaming, yes, that was it, Granny had just mentioned, 'sleep state' so she was asleep, only she so wished she wasn't. She needed to talk to her grandmother.*

'Granny, am I awake or asleep?'

'Your body's asleep, but *your mind* isn't, it doesn't sleep,' she said. *This was even more confusing.*

'Then which is … really me?' she asked, checking to see if she was still wearing her new Hollister PJs.

'The real you is your spirit or soul, and right now it's temporarily away from your body, here talking to me. Tatiana this *isn't* a dream.'

'My spirit? So, can the spirit remember everyone it's ever been?'

'Yes, in the mind, but when you're awake it's not possible to remember previous lifetimes, unless of course, you're extremely psychic.'

Ah! So it was possible – things were beginning to make sense. 'Granny, would Isabella remember me, feel—'

'She's in a time warp, so I don't know what she'd remember, but as for feelings, yes. It's strong emotions like fear and hate, even love, that stop ghosts from moving on.'

'And that's why Isabella's trapped?'

'Exactly, and why you have to release her.'

Tatiana slowly shook her head from side to side. 'I know, only how?'

Her grandmother held her hands up and shrugged. Tatiana frowned, *that wasn't much help, maybe she didn't know, or could the clue still lie with the picture?* She looked from her grandmother to Isabella's portrait and back again. 'Did strange things happen when it was here?'

'Yes. The picture made me uncomfortable to the point where

I felt compelled to do something about it. Your grandfather of course, thought I'd taken leave of my senses, but somehow I knew she hadn't died properly, that I had to help her; only that's easier said than done, as you'll discover. Then just as I thought I was getting somewhere, I became ill.'

Tatiana nodded; she knew only too well the unsettling effect the picture could have.

'Marcus and I *are* trying to find Isabella, but it's really difficult.'

'I know, but your psychic abilities, which are increasing all the time, will help, for unlike you, I wasn't psychic.'

Tatiana peered more closely at her grandmother, she appeared solid enough, but was she?

'Granny, are you a ghost or … what?'

'No!' she said, stifling a smile. '*I'm not earth-bound*! I'm just visiting my old home, not haunting the place. I come occasionally to see how your grandfather is doing.'

'It's so sad Grand-père can't see you too.'

'I know. We do meet up when he's asleep, only he doesn't remember. Which reminds me, I want you to do something else for me.'

Tatiana tried not to groan. 'Apart from rescuing Isabella?'

'Yes. Jacques's been fretting about a favourite tie he's lost. It's one I gave him on our last anniversary and I've watched him searching for it, getting more and more upset, but he won't find it because I took it to the cleaners shortly before I died and it's still there.'

'Poor Grand-père!'

'So I need *you* to tell him for me. He'll know which cleaners it is, then he can get it back.'

'No problem,' said Tatiana, relieved it wasn't anything more obscure. 'In exchange, please will you help us find Isabella?'

'Of course.'

Tatiana noticed her granny was becoming blurred around the

edges, and worried she'd vanish, asked, 'Then where is she?'

'I don't know exactly.'

'But you said you'd seen her.'

'Yes, well, I think I did, but only since I've been here and that was from a distance. She looked so wretched, and ill, not at all like she was in the picture. Her face was white and sunken, that lovely hair matted, uncombed and alive with lice, and her once beautiful clothes were ragged and quite filthy!'

'Was she in prison?'

'She had been, but then they moved her when the coughing got too bad.'

'Where to?'

'I don't know the name of the place, only how it looked over two hundred years ago, not how it is now.'

'*Granny*, that's no help!' she said.

'I will try and direct you ... to where I last—'

Tatiana could see right through her grandmother now and knew she'd soon be gone. 'But quickly, Granny, at least tell me how she died.'

'I don't know ... she was injured and—'

'*Granny*, you must help!' But too late, her grandmother was gone, along with the room and the portrait. Tatiana then jolted back to her senses to find herself in bed, wide-awake and freezing cold, with most of the duvet on the floor.

Next morning, Tatiana was longing to tell Marcus about her encounter with Granny Natasha, only with her mum in earshot she decided to wait until they were alone. Instead, she concentrated on working through the notebooks, while Marcus studied a street map of Paris. He located the area where the convent might be, on the left bank of the Seine, in easy walking distance of the apartment.

'Found anything?' asked Marcus.

'Her writing's really difficult to make out, but I'll try and translate some bits for you: "*Jacques doesn't approve, but I keep being drawn back to this place, it's as if something is pulling me here.*"'

'By "here" does she mean the chateau?'

'There's no way of knowing, because the pages are a jumble of random words, snatches of conversation or quotations she must have liked, but then here's another bit that might relate to Isabella: "*I thought I saw her again today … looking so sad, if only I knew how to help.*" What do you think of that?'

Marcus shrugged. 'She could be anyone, even a beggar in the street.'

'I know, but then there's something else that puzzles me,' she said, flipping to another page. 'Here, she mentions Ariadne, and that's not the only time, it might be a clue.'

'Ariadne?' muttered Marcus, rubbing his head.

'Greek mythology, you know, you must have done it at school! She helped Theseus slay the Minotaur and all that.'

Marcus rubbed his head harder. 'Yeah I remember, didn't she weave a web or something?'

'Not a web, she left a trail to help him find his way out of the place where the Minotaur lived.'

'*Tati,* is this really important?'

'It might be. Not the myth, but her references to it. Look here,' she said, pointing to the spidery writing. "*I could have saved myself a lot of time today if I'd followed Ariadne's example, instead I got lost and didn't find her.*" What's that mean?'

'Lost? Like where?'

'Doesn't say, but it kind of reminds me of my maze dream when I was lost and couldn't get out.'

'That's it!' shouted Marcus punching the air. 'Didn't the Minotaur live *underground* … in a labyrinth?'

Tatiana jumped to her feet. 'Of course! A maze, an underground maze … that's what we need to look for!'

'Do you think there's such a thing in Paris?' said Marcus thumbing through the guidebook. 'There's nothing in the index.'

Later that morning, Marcus and Tatiana wandered along the banks of the Seine past the bookstalls set up along the embankment, occasionally stopping to inspect a book or old print or idly lean on the wall and watch the boats go by. While Tatiana was telling Marcus what she could remember of her encounter with her grandmother, they saw a boat full of tourists pass under a bridge and as it disappeared around a bend in the river, Marcus remarked, 'That's how I think death is.'

'What do you mean?'

'Well, the boat is out of sight, *we* can no longer see it, but it's still there, just like when someone dies; they are still the same only *we* can't see them, like your grandmother.'

'Except as spirits.'

'That's different. So *are* you going to tell your grandfather about his tie?'

'I should, but he'll freak out, won't he?'

'Yup, what about telling your mum, let her do it?'

'Maybe, I don't know. Let's wait and see. The thing is granny will know if I don't and I did say I would. Now where is that convent?'

They found the church connected to the convent easily and, since it was open, wandered in. There were many plaques, detailing the people they commemorated and in many cases when and how they'd died. They ran their hands over the smooth cold marble effigies lying on top of raised tombs, fingered carved hands folded on chests and touched impassive white faces and pointed medieval feet resting on dogs. Nowhere was there a mention of Isabella. Leaving the church, they went in search of the graveyard, which they assumed must be nearby, but it wasn't, just buildings and cobbles and concrete everywhere. Marcus urged Tatiana to ask someone.

She glanced around at the few meandering shoppers before deciding to return to the church. 'Hang on while I find a priest,' she said.

Tatiana reappeared a few minutes later shaking her head. 'That's that then,' she said, sinking onto a nearby bench. 'They've all gone.'

'What's gone?'

'The graves – *two hundred* years ago!' she said, tugging her jacket tighter around her and pulling her woolly hat down over her ears. 'He said many of the graveyards, including the one near here called the Cemetery of the Innocents, were cleared for building around the time of the Revolution.'

'What about the convent?' he asked.

'That's no good either. The nuns moved to the country during the war.'

'What do you suppose happened to all the remains from the cemeteries?'

'The priest said the bones had been moved.'

'Did he say where?'

'Yes, the Catacombs, in the underground quarries left by the Romans.'

'So she must be there.'

'We could see if you like, it's open to the public, only the priest looked at me like I was crazy when I said I was hoping to find someone.'

'We must go, Tati, it sounds like our best hope.'

'Marcus, he said there were *millions* of bones!'

'Great!'

'Bones it is then,' said Tatiana, unfolding the map again.

Chapter 9

Ossuary

Marcus and Tatiana emerged from the Metro at Denfert-Rochereau and made their way across the square to an inconspicuous green door, the entrance to the Catacombs. After purchasing a guidebook and tickets from a sallow-faced man, more intent on reading the newspaper and picking his teeth than attending to them, they began the twenty-metre descent below ground by a narrow spiral staircase. They corkscrewed steeply downwards, deeper and deeper into the earth, until arriving at the bottom, where they entered a small room containing an illustrated history of the Catacombs.

'Get a load of this,' said Tatiana reading from one of the displays. 'It says the hollowed-out galleries we're about to see were the former subterranean limestone quarries used for the building of Paris, and the galleries are on *three* different levels.'

'And here it says the tunnels are named after the streets above them – clever, saves you getting lost.'

'That's just it, people *did* get lost. It says that one man never found his way out and his remains weren't found till *years* later!

'Well we're not likely to get lost, because only a small section of the galleries are open to the public.'

'Just as well since it says that the ossuary covers over eleven thousand square metres, that's gigantic!'

'Ossuary?'

'Yes, a place containing human bones it says, and listen to this, "*During the Revolution and for many years afterwards people hid in the Catacombs, too frightened of what was taking place above ground to come out.*"'

'Escaping the Terror and beheadings of the Commune.'

'In that case Isabella could have lived and died right *here*!'

'*Exactly!* Underground like the Minotaur.'

Hearing other people descending the staircase, they decided to get going. On leaving the exhibition rooms they entered a very long, narrow passage that ran straight for as far as they could see. They set off along the dimly lit tunnel at a fast walk. The damp gravel scrunched underfoot and the low roof dripped icy dollops of water on their heads. Once they stopped to look back, but could see nothing, just the tunnel disappearing into a point of darkness in both directions.

'I'm not too sure about this,' muttered Tatiana. 'Shall we go back?'

'No way! We haven't seen any bones yet,' said Marcus, grabbing her hand.

After walking for several more minutes the tunnel opened out into a wide area encircled by square pillars painted in striking black and white geometric patterns. Facing them was a similarly decorated doorway with an inscription above reading: '*Arrête! C'est ici l'Empire de la Mort.*'

'What's it say, Tati?'

'"*Halt! You are entering the Empire of Death.*" You still on for this?' she said, suppressing a shiver.

'You bet,' said Marcus.

Once inside the ossuary they saw plaques set into the walls.

'Look, these inscriptions say which cemetery the bones came from,' said Marcus, 'and the date they were moved here.'

Then they saw them. Bones, bones and yet more bones. The walls were built entirely from bones. Thighbones formed intricate criss-cross patterns in some sections, in others only sculls had been used and yet others were made from decorative combinations of bones. Behind these artistically formed walls other, smaller, miscellaneous bones had been thrown haphazardly into the back of the deep galleries, piled in towering mounds of jagged human remains.

'It's incredible,' gasped Tatiana, her eyes opening wider and wider as they continued walking through gallery after gallery. 'No wonder the priest shook his head at me. There's no hope whatsoever of finding an individual skeleton.'

'No, but at least we're on the right track, because this plaque says that these bones were brought from the Carmes convent in the Place Maubert on 25th January 1814. So there we have it!'

'Then she could be amongst these,' said Tatiana swinging her arm in a wide arc.

They continued on until the narrow winding path they were following ended in a round opening with a pool in the centre. A plaque stated that the surrounding walls were made from the bones brought from the Cemetery of the Innocents.

'These bones are also from the right area, not that it's much help.'

'No, besides, I don't see why a spirit would want to stick around a load of dusty old bones, it's probably not even haunted down here.'

'You'd think all these gloomy passages and millions of bones would make it creepy, but somehow it's not.'

'I don't see what's scary about bones—' Marcus was saying when he stopped and emitted an excited whoop. 'This has to be it! Ariadne's underground labyrinth.'

Tatiana stared at him. 'Of course! This was where Granny saw Isabella. At last!'

They were wandering along chatting when they heard voices approaching.

'Come on, Tati, we don't want to get caught up with a load of tourists,' said Marcus diving down an ill-lit tunnel. They hurried along the path past inscribed tablets, ornate tombs, niches and tiny rooms until it opened into a small square punctuated by pillars.

'Look at all these skulls!' gasped Tatiana.

'We can't look now, that group's catching up with us,' said Marcus.

He pulled Tatiana down behind a pillar made exclusively from sculls, where they sat hidden from sight and waited while the guide droned on in Japanese. Even after the party had moved through, Marcus and Tatiana remained leaning against the pillar, their shoulders lightly touching. After a few minutes he handed her his scarf to cushion her back from the scull's sharp edges.

'Thanks, Marcus, that's much better,' she murmured, wriggling into a more comfortable position. And so they remained absorbed in a thought-filled silence amidst the unheard whispers of the countless dead. Marcus was still miles away when Tatiana felt a chilly sensation sweep through her.

'I'm frozen,' she whispered.

'Shall we go then?'

'No. The cold's from something ... *other,* and I can hear someone singing.'

'Singing! I can't.'

'Shut your eyes and try,' she said.

As Marcus closed his eyes, a shivery sensation shot through him. 'I can feel something, but can't hear anything.'

'I can, childish voices, all faint and echo-y,' she murmured in a faraway voice.

'Are they...?'

'I think so, although I *can see* them,' she said, pointing towards a pillar.

Tatiana watched as two young girls emerged cautiously from behind the pillar opposite. 'Two girls and they're singing my song!' exclaimed Tatiana. Craning forward, she watched the girls skipping and leaping around in a circle, until for no apparent reason, they fell on ground giggling, before getting up and starting all over again.

'They're playing,' she whispered, 'and they have bare feet. They must be so cold. A small boy has joined them ... he's pointing at us!'

This was different from 'it' in the drawing room; she could see them; they were whole and looked as real and natural as if they were alive. *She couldn't be afraid of these young children, could she?* Holding her breath, she slowly knelt and extended a hand towards the three puzzled faces, encouraging them to come closer. They didn't move and she was sure they'd disappear at any second when the tallest, a girl in a brown floor-length dress, smiled and beckoned for her to join in their game.

Tatiana didn't dare move. 'What's that song?' she asked softly.

The children huddled together; then burst into uncertain laughter before inching closer. Tatiana decided to try another approach and began, in a haltering voice, to sing an improvised verse from the poem with 'her' same tune.

"Three ghostly *listeners,*

...stood listening ... just like you ...

to voices from another time..."

'Mais non!' exclaimed the eldest girl, drawing closer. *'Ce n'est pas comme ça.'*

Then she sang the song again and when she'd finished, bobbed a curtsey to Tatiana and said, *'C'est intitulé "La Gentille et Jeune Lisette," mademoiselle.'* Tatiana's heart leapt at the mention of that name again; it seemed to be cropping up all over the place, rather like her tune.

'Marcus,' she said, 'my tune's real – it's called, "The Sweet and Young Lisette!" Isn't that amazing?'

Marcus looked at Tatiana, who'd shut her eyes. 'Have they gone?'

'No, by concentrating, I can still see them in my head, just,' she murmured.

Marcus ran his hands through his hair and slumped back against the pillar. 'Find out what they're doing down here.' But there was no need for Tatiana to ask, because the children had already picked up on his thoughts.

'The shy, middle one, said, *"Notre père est mort,"* like their father's dead, killed during the Terror. They're waiting for it to end.'

'Tell them it's over,' said Marcus.

'I did,' said Tatiana, 'but the boy said the girls can't leave; they're waiting for their mother to fetch them. She told them to hide if anyone came and not to make a sound. That's why they've taken their shoes off.'

Then addressing the three curious faces, she asked, 'What do you do all day?'

'We play, and wait for Maman,' said one.

'And they watch the people in funny clothes, like you, who speak with strange words,' said the small boy, pressing his hand over his mouth, but not before Tatiana saw the gap between his small white teeth. A sensation, she hadn't felt since leaving home, started welling inside her. She clutched her stomach. *No! She would not panic.*

'Find out what year it is,' said Marcus, 'and which king—' He'd hardly finished speaking when the eldest girl raised her head and proudly announced, 'It is 1794 and there is no king. He is dead.'

The smaller of the two girls smiled despondently at Tatiana and said, 'Maman said she would fetch us. Sometimes we see her faintly in the distance, but she never comes close and when we run towards her, she always disappears, so we have to stay here and wait.'

As she spoke, Tatiana noticed the children beginning to dissolve. Her eyes shot open. 'Marcus! They must be stuck, we have to rescue the poor things.'

'Come off it, Tati! We can't rescue every stranded ghost we encounter, anyway how?'

'Don't know, Granny never said, but be should try … just in case.'

'*If* we ever find her,' said Marcus, looking wildly around, 'so what do you suggest?'

'First I'll have to explain to them about being dead; then we'll try leading them out, and once they're above ground they'll see all the changes, cars and things.'

'But will they? They may see everything as it was in their time, like your grandmother does.'

'They can see us,' said Tatiana.

'Maybe because we're spiritual beings like them, not inanimate structural things ... there's only one way to find out, Tati...'

'Okay. I'll explain, only they do seem to find my modern French very funny.'

'What about telepathy?'

'*That's it*, we'll do it, together.'

'Okay, you visualize them, and we'll both concentrate, mentally explaining about them being dead and not having bodies,' whispered Marcus.

'And tell them they're free and don't need to stay here anymore,' Tatiana added.

'Yes, and only if that doesn't work, will we try leading them out of here.'

'That sounds kind of all right, not that I'm convinced it will work.'

'Me neither.'

'Should we say a prayer?' asked Tatiana.

'*Pray?*'

'Yes, to light beings, you know, angels and things, to help.'

'*Angels?*'

Tatiana believed in such things, but not sure if Marcus did, just nodded.

'You can if you like, and better ask your grandmother to help too while you're about it,' he added.

They both sank to their knees. After several minutes of intense concentration, Tatiana opened her eyes and peered around at the seemingly empty galleries. The mistiness had gone along with the chill in her back. 'I can't see them anymore,' she whispered.

'Do you think they've gone?'

'I don't know, but since they aren't here now, we might as well go too.'

Chapter 10

Outer Dimensions, Inner Worlds

Rush hour was in full swing when Marcus and Tatiana, feeling like two squashed sardines, emerged from the crowded Metro at Concorde. But instead of heading for the apartment they turned in the opposite direction so Marcus could visit the infamous Place de la Concorde. The huge square, jammed with drivers all anxious to get home, made reaching the area, where the guillotine once stood, somewhat hazardous.

'That was a bit hairy,' exclaimed Marcus, after they'd made it across in a blast of car horns. Once there, they found the spot was marked by no more than a simple brass memorial near the base of a soaring Egyptian obelisk flanked by two ornate fountains.

'Is this all?' asked Tatiana, looking at the dull and factual plaque commemorating those who'd lost their lives during the Revolution.

Tatiana sat on the edge of the fountain squinting at Marcus. 'Before we go, I'm going to close my eyes and see what happens.'

'Isn't it getting a bit late for that stuff?' he asked, squatting beside her.

'Just once more,' she said, patting the ground beside her. 'I might see the guillotine or even Isabella.'

Marcus wrinkled his nose. 'Here, in the middle of all this noise and traffic?'

'Why not?' she said. 'This is the very spot where all those people lost their lives.'

Not wanting to argue, Marcus lowered himself down beside her, and twiddling his thumbs, prepared to wait.

Tatiana, trying to ignore the penetrating cold of the paving stones, stretched out her legs, pulled her hat over her ears, and leaning back against the fountain wall, stared up at the point of the obelisk where the gold pyramid-shaped peak merged into the evening sky. She pulled the box containing Isabella's hair from her pocket and clutching it, shut her eyes against the reflected glare of the lowering sun. After a few moments of deep breathing a dreamy relaxation began to steal over her, the drone of tyres spinning over cobbles morphed into the sound of steel thudding into wood and she found herself spiralling dizzily through a vortex of all-encompassing darkness, back to a succession of increasingly earlier points in time.

Where the obelisk had stood seconds before, she now saw the guillotine, a rough wooden scaffold holding the deadly blade, the bench where the condemned person would be strapped down, and, *was that a severed head lying in the blood-soaked basket beneath the blade*? She looked closer – *how horrible! This wasn't what she'd expected to see.* The whole grisly apparatus stood on a raised platform, a stage no less, so the spectacle of death could be shared with the bloodthirsty citizens of the Revolution. She was wishing the guillotine would disappear, when her attention was drawn to a tall figure in the surrounding crowd. There was something about him that made him seem out of place; nothing definable, but even with his hat pulled down over his face, she could tell he wasn't as rough as the other spectators. Also, there was a familiarity about him. *Was he someone she knew, in disguise perhaps? Yes, that must be it, for his clothes, although shabby, were far too well cut and his hair, tied with a black ribbon at the nape of his neck, was clean*. She was puzzling over whom the man might be when their eyes met and grimacing the man shook his head. *What was that meant to mean?*

The clang of steel pummelling the chateau's massive wrought iron gates soon gave way to a short outburst of cheering punctuated by several high-pitched screams. Lisette, who was crossing the hall with André, came to an abrupt halt. *What was that? Had the villagers, who they knew so well, and had always cared for, really dared to invade the chateau*? Then she heard the unmistakable rhythmic thump of soldiers marching, a sound that made her heart pound in her ears. *Where was everyone? Where were all the servants, her maman?* She was still pondering when André seized her hand and dragging her behind him, bounded up the curving staircase and along the passage to the ornately gilded doors leading to the main rooms. Without pausing, he threw them open with such force that the doors were left quivering on their hinges.

'Henriette! Countess! Where are you?' he shouted, sprinting from one interconnecting room to another. It wasn't until they burst unceremoniously into her maman's boudoir, André with his coat tails flying, that they found the women, engaged in a noisy game of chance.

'What is this unseemly outburst André, Lisette?' cried Isabella, fanning herself with her cards. 'Lud, Sir, you look as if you've taken fright! Why I do declare your wig is missing, and as for your hair, Lisette, well it quite stands on end!'

'Hell's teeth, this is no time for formalities,' she heard André mutter, as he made a cursory bow.

'Forgive me, Madame, but you are in mortal danger and must leave this moment – all of you!' he said, trying to keep his voice steady and not shout. Henriette immediately jumped to her feet and clasped Lisette to her, but Isabella, although visibly paling under her thick white make-up, remained seated.

'Don't be so dramatic, André,' she said, laughing. 'Leave! Why I have no intention of going anywhere. Philippe has assured me it is quite safe in the country.'

'You have to, now,' he said, appealing to Henriette. 'Members of the Revolutionary Guard are here and'—he didn't want to scare them more than necessary—'the rabble who were outside the gates earlier will undoubtedly follow them in. It is only a question of time. If the Guards don't take you, they will. We must make our escape, now, while we can.'

Lisette, who'd been standing quietly, broke free from Henriette and grabbed her mother's hands. 'Come, Maman, please we have to go,' she cried.

'Certainly not. We're not going to *run away,*' said Isabella, haughtily.

'Then we'll all stay, be taken together,' said André, through clenched teeth.

'No! Take Lisette and Henriette. Keep Lisette safe for me. When the soldiers have left and all is well, come and tell me André, for I'll be here waiting for you,' she said, with a fluttering of eyelashes. Then dismissing them with a wave of her fan, she scooped her small dog, *Anais,* from the ground and kissed it.

Seeing her maman was determined to stay, Lisette allowed herself to be shepherded towards the door by André. 'Don't fret, I'll come back for her,' he whispered.

He opened the door a fraction to make sure it was safe. The adjoining room, Isabella's bedchamber, was empty, but the sounds reverberating from below left them in no doubt that the soldiers were already inside, leaving them few options for escape. *They'd have to hide, but where?* Lisette's mind was racing with possibilities. 'I know a hiding place, somewhere Papa showed me when I was little.' she said. 'No one knows about it, not even Maman, it was our secret.'

'Hiding's no good; we must get away from here, to a place of safety. What about the horses?' said Henriette.

'Too late, the mob will most certainly have made off with them by now,' said André, opening the door. 'Come now Lisette, show us this secret place of yours, and Madame, lock the door and make sure you barricade it with furniture.'

The three of them stood listening. The banging doors and raised voices coming from the floor below were louder now, then they heard a sound that sent shafts of fear though them – heavy boots on the main staircase. *They were too late; they'd be seized, thrown in prison and…*

'Quick, Lisette, which way?' hissed André.

Without a word, she removed her shoes, motioned for them to do the same and hoisting her skirts, pointed at the tapestries covering the far wall. He nodded, grimacing. *She could tell he wasn't convinced, after all, the entire household knew about the concealed door, it was hardly a secret, but he'd have to trust her.* Holding a finger to her lips, she beckoned for them to follow.

Carrying their shoes, they ran soundlessly across the polished floor, slithering to a halt beside the heavily draped four-poster bed. André pulled back a section of tapestry, opened the small service door behind it, saw the others through and closed it behind them. They crept silently down a narrow spiral staircase to an underground passage at the bottom, where André turned to Lisette, and craning to see her expression in the half-light, asked, 'Now where?' She bit her lip. *Could she really remember where to go after all these years*? And if *she couldn't they'd be trapped; there was no way out from here.* 'The cellars,' she whispered.

'Are you sure?'

She nodded and mouthed, 'At the very far end, behind the barrels in an arched recess there's a slate, it's a trapdoor to a cavern, but it will be very dark and difficult to find without candles.'

'Besides no candles, we have no key,' muttered André, as he inspected the empty lock in the stout, handless door facing them.

For a moment a worried frown flashed across Lisette's face; then her eyes brightened, and she sank to her knees and started probing the lower edge of the wall with her fingertips. André and Henriette were watching helplessly, when there was a slight movement beneath her hands, and there in a crevice between the bricks, she felt the smooth barrel of a key. 'Voilà!'

Tatiana thought she'd returned to normal, but as her eyes opened onto darkness and the overpowering smell of dank musty stone, she knew she was still there, crawling out of the cavern with Henriette and André.

'How long do you think we've been down here?' asked Lisette, as André grabbed her unceremoniously under the arms and hauled her through the trapdoor in the floor.

'Two days, maybe more, it's difficult to gauge the passage of time in the dark,' he said, reaching down to help Henriette.

'Well the cramps and grumblings in my stomach tell me it must have been all of that and more,' said Lisette, as they fumbled their way through the pitch-black cellars. André fished in his pocket for the key and released them back into the dimly lit passage. Screwing up her eyes, Lisette blinked and staggered sideways grabbing at the wall for support. After consuming nothing other than sips of wine for days, they were all light-headed and wobbled precariously as they crept cautiously along the passage. Passing the empty kitchens, they went up the back stairs to the ground floor and continued on through the silent chateau. Every room they entered had been ransacked, hit by a vicious wave of wanton destruction, not a single servant in sight. When they reached her maman's room and found her gone, her beloved dog cowering under an up-tuned chair, the days of Lisette's carefree childhood came to an abrupt end.

'*Maman! Maman! Where are you*?' she shrieked.

André tried to restrain her, but she wriggled free and ran off. She ran on and on through the chateau searching in every conceivable place for her maman until coming to what was left of her own bedchamber, where, overcome by a sickening feeling of hopelessness, she slumped onto the window seat. As she gazed out of the window at the sight of the travelling coach lying on its side in the courtyard below, the door emblazoned with the family coat of arms, wrenched off and despoiled on the ground nearby, she found herself slipping back to a much happier time.

Lisette sighed, a sigh that became longer and more contented the further she leant from the window. She felt no inclination to run down to greet the new arrivals; the formalities of curtseying and bowing could wait. For now she wanted to watch, unobserved, the passengers alighting from the coach, delight in seeing her dearest half-sister, Cécile, and feast her eyes on the dashing young man she could see still astride his sweating horse. From the safety of her eyrie she could observe the Chevalier Pellerin as much as she liked without her manners being deemed improper by Henriette.

Her gaze lingered dreamily on Henri Pellerin. She could hardly believe her luck, that her Papa had engaged such a handsome new secretary. Cécile had already extolled his virtues to her, telling her of his past career as a cavalry officer, his brilliant connections and razor sharp wit and how he was quite the fashion in Paris, popular amongst all who knew him, particularly the ladies.

She slipped down from the window seat and hugging herself, twirled around her room humming.

'Lisette, what are you doing? The party's arrived from Versailles and look at you!' exclaimed Henriette, bursting in on her thoughts.

'And Cécile and Henri…' she said.

'Yes, of course, you've been so eager to see everyone I thought you would have been outside to greet them.'

'I'll go now.'

'Not until you've changed your dress and your hair has been arranged,' said Henriette, ringing the bell to summons Marie, Lisette's maid.

'Must I? They will be in their travelling clothes and—'

'Lisette, your maman will not like to see you so plainly dressed, she will think I let you run wild when she is away.'

Lisette smiled sweetly and put an arm around Henriette's waist. Yes, she would allow herself to be dressed as befitted a young lady, not that she was, quite, for at barely thirteen she was still firmly in the schoolroom. And Marie could tame her hair, but it wasn't for Maman or her Papa's sake – she had other reasons for wanting to look pretty ... and more grown up.

'Now before you go down, Lisette you must remember, for I told you last time he was here, not to make a nuisance of yourself, bothering the Chevalier—'

'But I don't, Mademoiselle Henriette! Why, he hardly acknowledges my existence and only ever speaks to me if I ask him something in particular about literature,' she said, and feeling her cheeks flush, turned away.

'That's what I mean, you pester him with questions, especially when he is talking to Cécile.'

'But it's not fair that I should have to keep quiet, she sees him at court and I never see anyone exciting, only you and Monsieur Imertinsky.'

'When you are older, you'll go to court too,' said Henriette, suppressing a smile.

Lisette pulled a long face. 'The Queen was married when little older than me.'

'Yes, for political reasons, to a man she didn't even know. Now go down and make your greetings.'

She was about to leave when she noticed Henriette's uneasy expression. 'Is something wrong?' she asked.

Henriette shook her head before saying, ' Not wrong exactly, not yet. I didn't want to alarm you, Lisette, but your father, and the Chevalier have only escorted your mother and Cécile to Clèrmency to make sure they got here safely. They will be returning to Paris almost immediately, where the unrest that's been brewing for months has now reached boiling point and become openly menacing.'

Tatiana smiled, and yawning, opened her eyes to see Marcus looking pinched and uncomfortable. 'You okay?' she asked.

'Sort of, but my bum's frozen to the ground,' he said. And

jumping to his feet, rubbed his backside.

'You should have said so.'

'What and disturb you? So, did you see anything interesting?'

'Yes, and wow! Was that something! She said turning to Marcus. 'It was incredible.'

'You must tell me, but not here, it's nearly dark,' he said, and reaching down helped her up.

Tatiana nodded; she couldn't stop thinking about Lisette's crush on the gorgeous Henri Pellerin. 'Yes, besides we need to get home before Mum completely freaks out.'

When they got back to the apartment Tatiana's mum was busy in the kitchen preparing dinner whilst her grand-père read the papers by the fire in the sitting room. As predicted, their prolonged absence, exacerbated by Tatiana's lack of communication had sent her mum into a towering rage. Not only that, she demanded a full account of how they'd spent the day, but first, she told her that her dad had rung and he wanted her to call back. *Oh no! What had she done now?*

She picked up the phone and dialled and it was answered almost immediately. 'Dad?'

'Ah, Tatiana ... about your behaviour...' Her heart sank, another lecture on her manners, why did he have to be so impossibly old-fashioned? 'For goodness sake, Tatiana, you're not ten...'

'That's just it,' she snapped, her eyes blazing. 'You don't understand; neither of you do; why can't you let me grow up ... be me, not some puppet of yours?'

'*Tatiana! How dare you!*' he exploded. But she'd gone too far to stop now and to hell with the consequences.

'You and Mum treat me like I'm a child. How can I behave like a grown-up when neither of you let me make decisions for myself. Even my clothes are an issue with you disapproving of anything I like. How do you think that makes me feel? And even with Marcus here Mum can't relax and let us go off and have fun without fussing all the time, she's—' She heard a sharp intake of breath on the other end of the line followed by a deafening silence. *Now she'd done it. Suppose he ordered her home – like immediately?*

'Tatiana!' The tone in which he spat out her name told her that his lips were pressed into a hard line. She could hear him breathing, but he didn't speak, which was almost more intimidating than being yelled at. *No.* She glared at the telephone. *She could play that game too, and if he was waiting for an apology, well he could wait. She'd meant every word she'd said.*

Finally, he spoke. 'Listen to me, Tati. You know perfectly well your mother worries when you go off on your own at home, never mind a huge city like Paris. Why can't you just call her, let her know you're safe instead of disappearing for hours on end.'

Surprised by his conciliatory tone, Tatiana gulped. 'I would, only my mobile doesn't really work here and when it does, it gobbles up my credit.'

'For *Gods sake,* Tati, you're fourteen going on fifteen, sort it out – go and buy a French Sim card!'

Tatiana went back to the kitchen and grinning sheepishly, apologised to her mum. That wasn't so bad; maybe she should try standing up to her dad more often.

'You went down the Catacombs! *Whatever for?*' her mum exclaimed. 'I really don't like the thought of you going to such sinister places, all those horrible old bones.'

'Actually it was fascinating, Mum.'

'The bones from the old cemeteries were moved there, so we went to try and find Isabella's,' said Marcus.

'And did you?' asked her grandfather peering quizzically over the top of his spectacles.

'Difficult to say,' said Marcus, 'since there were literally millions of them.'

Tatiana's mum shuddered and frowned. 'If you're really so

interested in her, wouldn't it be better to visit places she'd have known and put an end to this morbid searching for skeletons and graves?' she asked.

'But of course,' her grandfather said. 'We should take the children to the country – drive out to Versailles, show them where Marie Antoinette and Louis XVI held court.'

'What about the chateau at Clèrmency, where Granny used to go?' asked Tatiana.

'Shh, Tati, Your grandfather will *never* take you there.'

'Why not? They're family aren't they and Granny Natasha went?'

'She did, only she never made contact with the family.'

'Why? Don't they like us?'

'Well, it's a bit silly, something to do with their side of the family claiming possession of the chateau after the Revolution when it should have been returned to Philippe's side.'

'But that was centuries ago!'

'I know, but when my grandparents came to France and found the present Lafonts living there, they felt so strongly about it, they wouldn't even talk to them. All quite ridiculous! Especially as the only survivor of the family at the time was Lisette who was married and living in Russia.'

'If that's all, then surely we could go, like Granny did, when it's open to the public?'

Her mum shook her head and after a quick look at Tatiana's grandfather, who seemed absorbed in the paper, whispered, 'I think my mother would have liked to re-establish the connection, but your grandfather, who's not even a blood relation, wouldn't hear of it and so the silly feud goes on.'

'Quite right,' snapped her grandfather, thumping his paper. 'Bloody usurpers, you should be living there, not them! Forget the chateau, tomorrow we'll go to Versailles.'

Chapter 11

Here, There or Where?

The following morning, when Marcus still hadn't appeared for breakfast, Tatiana banged loudly on his door. 'You've got to get up, Marcus – *now*.'

'I can't.'

'Why not? Are you sick?' she asked, prodding the mound under the duvet.

'No. I had a nightmare and I'm exhausted!' he said, burrowing deeper under the quilt.

'Oh, just a dream.'

'It wasn't *just a dream,* it was important.'

'Okay, so an important one, but we have to go to the country soon, so you'd better get up,' she said, going to the door.

'No, stop,' he called. 'We have to go back to the Catacombs today – I dreamt the children hadn't gone.'

Tatiana swivelled, hands on hips. 'Grand-père and Mum have arranged the trip for today, and he hates having his plans altered, so get dressed. We'll see about the children tomorrow.'

'But we must—'

'*Marcus,* after two hundred years of being stuck, one more day isn't going to make any difference,' she snapped.

'Tati, what's the matter?'

'Nothing.'

'There is,' he said, emerging from under the bedclothes. 'I can tell, you're all spiky.'

'No I'm not. I'm fine.'

'Come off it, Tati, you know you're not,' he said, in a gentler tone.

'I told them about Granny and the tie,' she said, kicking at a trainer lying on the floor. 'I should have kept my mouth shut because now Grand-père's gone ominously quiet, Mum's mad at me, and you're making it worse by not getting up, and it seems that's my fault too!'

Marcus noticed her brimming eyes. 'Why didn't you say so before, instead of spitting at me?'

'What's the point? It *was* my fault.'

'No it wasn't, I would have done the same.'

'Grand-père didn't say anything, but his jaw was tightly clenched and he looked so mournful. Mum was furious that I'd upset him, said it was bad for his heart and might make him ill again.'

'Don't worry, it'll blow over.'

'But Mum accused me of making things up, lying. She said I was fantasising, that it was all in my mind,' she said, biting her lip.

Marcus swung his legs out of bed and taking Tatiana in his arms, gave her a quick hug.

'Forget it, Tati.'

'Hurry and get dressed then … and I can't wait to hear about your nightmare. I really mean it,' she murmured, giving his shoulder an encouraging squeeze.

Marcus beamed. 'Give me two minutes and I'll be ready'

Her mum pulled into a parking space outside a row of shops and, ordering Marcus and Tatiana to wait in the car with her grandfather, went to collect his medication from the pharmacy. After a few moments of sitting in silence her grandfather also got out of the car, muttering about reminding her mum about something. Tatiana offered to chase after her for him, but he said he wanted to go himself. They had just begun discussing Marcus's nightmare about the children, when her mum opened the car door and got in.

'Where's your grandfather?' she asked.

'Didn't he find you?'

'No. I haven't seen him,' she said pursing her lips. 'You shouldn't have let him go, heaven knows where he's gone now.'

'He insisted,' said Marcus. 'We could *hardly* have stopped him.'

'I'll have to search the shops,' said her mum, opening the car door. 'He's become so absent-minded recently that he might even have got a bus home!'

'No, it's all right,' said Tatiana, pointing to a bent figure emerging from a music shop. 'He's coming back.'

'*What on earth* was he doing in there?' exclaimed her mum.

Tatiana's grandfather got into the front seat clutching two plastic bags tightly to his chest, a secretive smile twitching about his lips.

'Well! What are you waiting for, Katya?' he said, rounding on her. 'Let's get going.'

Tatiana's mum shot an exasperated glance at her father, barked at Marcus and Tatiana to put on their seat belts, and they were off.

Forty-five minutes after leaving the traffic-clogged streets of Paris they reached Versailles. Her grandfather had been telling Marcus and Tatiana about the Chateau and was recounting the part it had played in French history, culminating in the bloody Revolution, when he turned to Tatiana.

'Plenty of ghosts for you to talk to here,' he said, raising one eyebrow and fixing her with a curious look.

'Oh? she stammered, trying not to catch her mum's eye. 'It was only a dream, Grand-père, and I—'

'No more of this silly talk, Tatiana; now then, where shall we start?'

They were walking across the car park towards the Chateau when her grandfather stopped to look at his watch.

'Did I tell you we're expected for lunch at one o'clock?' he said.

'*Lunch!* Where?'

'With the Lafonts. When I telephoned this morning, they asked us, so kind, don't you think?'

'But you don't like them!' her mum gasped.

'No, I don't, but then I've never met them,' he said, ruefully. 'And then I thought how pleased Natasha would be if the young people saw the old place, and—'

Hardly able to believe what he was saying, they all stared speechlessly at him as her mum mumbled under her breath, '*Lunch* at Clèrmency! *Why* didn't you say so before? We should have gone straight there. Then flashing her father a baleful look, added, 'Now we're going to be late.'

'*Mais non.*'

'*Mais oui*, it's many kilometres from here *and* I don't know the way,' she snapped, bundling everyone back into the car. With a grinding of gears, they set off once more. While her mum drove, her grandfather, seemingly oblivious to the trouble he'd caused, kept Marcus and Tatiana amused with anecdotes about the family and house they were going to visit.

'So the Lafonts are sort of cousins,' said Tatiana.

'Yes, but the branch of the family who live there now were remote cousins even back then.'

'We're hardly related then?'

'Well it's very distant, although your grandmother liked to refer to them as cousins.'

After a particularly frightening drive with her mum forgetting where she was and hurtling round corners on the wrong side of the road, overtaking at random and generally driving much too fast, they arrived at the chateau. The moment they passed through the front gates Tatiana broke out in a cold sweat.

'Mum! *Stop the car.*'

'What is it?'

'I don't feel well.'

'Oh no! Tati, not now!'

Tatiana threw open the door and leapt out. Once she felt better, she glanced nervously at the imposing house in the distance. Glimpsed through the trees flanking the winding drive, the chateau looked large and imposing. She could see conical turrets at the corners and how the panes of glass in the symmetrical lines of windows shone in the sunlight, making it look as if they were lit from within. She got back in the car, suddenly overcome by a terrifying excitement. *Could this grand place really have been her family home?*

'I expect it was the journey that made you ill,' grandfather Jacques said, 'enough to make someone with the strongest of constitutions seasick.'

'This is a car not a boat,' spat her mum. 'If you'd told me we were coming here in the first place there'd have been no need to drive so fast, *and* we'd be properly dressed for the occasion.'

They parked at the front of the chateau and got out. Her grandfather pulled on the bell rope hanging by the front door and straightened his tie while her mum made an attempt at finger-combing Tatiana's wayward hair.

'*Mum*!'

Tatiana held her breath as the weathered door swung open, only to release it when a blousy middle-aged woman with faded blonde hair and too much lipstick stepped out. She was not what she'd been expecting. The woman ushered them into a freezing hall where their shoes clattered on the marble tiles and their breath billowed dragon-like before them. They then followed her up a curving staircase to the first floor, through two interconnecting rooms until arriving at a pair of gilded doors, where the housekeeper stood aside and motioned for them to enter.

One glance at the library was all Tatiana needed to confirm the tumult coursing through her veins. Her mum drew herself up to her full height and swept in to greet her unknown relatives with an exaggerated show of warmth and affection.

'Hello, Jacques, Katya, welcome, a welcome long overdue, *non*?' said Monsieur Lafont, extending both hands in greeting. Tatiana stared at her distant relation with an ill-disguised curiosity observing his immaculate manners and confident air as he put them at ease.

'Indeed,' replied her grandfather, 'so very good of you to allow us to bring the young people to meet you and see your beautiful home.'

'The family home, your family too, you should have come a long time ago,' Monsieur Lafont said, shaking hands formally with Marcus; he then kissed Tatiana's hand, as he had her mum's, and as he did she noticed a flash of ill-suppressed mirth cross Marcus's face.

'What do you think of the old place?' he enquired, as he poured drinks for them all.

Before anyone had time to answer an elegant, stern-faced woman with a distinctly long nose, entered the room. One look from her unsmiling eyes as she greeted them was enough. She didn't know why, but Madame Lafont's disdainful air made her jittery and a feeling of totally inadequacy swept over her.

'Je m'excuse, I am so sorry, I was seeing to lunch. Marie is not as particular as me,' she explained, after formally introducing herself. 'Now, would anyone like to use the bathroom after the journey?' Everyone shook their heads with the exception of Tatiana who was still feeling decidedly wobbly.

'Yes please,' she said.

'Come, I'll show you the way,' said Madame Lafont.

'No need, I know where it is,' said Tatiana, dashing to the door.

'How does she?' asked her mum, who was looking at their hostess, who merely blinked and gave an indifferent shrug.

Tatiana ran lightly back to the top of the stairs, turned left off the landing and headed down a corridor. After a few paces she stopped to look around. She was sure there should have been a door, right here where she was standing, but there wasn't and that puzzled her. Maybe she was wrong. She moved on more slowly until coming to a closed door on the left. She stopped, and was wondering if her intuition was right and she dared go in, when it flew open and a young man rushed out in such haste that he nearly bowled her over. For interminable seconds they remained fixed to the spot, virtually touching and so close she could feel the warmth of his breath on her face. His brown eyes consumed her with such intensity that Tatiana, feeling her face go crimson, was forced to step back. Her eyes faltered and momentarily she looked away.

'I'm so sorry!' she stuttered. 'I was … looking for the bathroom.'

'Mais non, pardonnez-mois,' he said. 'It is I who am being sorry,' he repeated, hesitantly correcting himself in English. 'I nearly did knock you flat down.'

Tatiana, smiling at his quaint English, held out her hand. 'You must be my sort of cousin, I'm Tatiana,' she said in immaculate French.

'And I'm Louis,' he said. 'Come, I will show you to my bathroom if you will excuse the untidiness of the bedchamber.' He led her through his bedroom, Tatiana hardly daring to look, and indicated his bathroom. Tatiana hurriedly thanked him.

Alone in his bathroom, she clasped her hands to her thumping chest. *'Oh wow! Wow, wow wow!'* she whispered to her flushed reflection in the basin mirror. 'That was so weird and … *what's* happening?' She shook her head, her hair flying back and forth slapping her cheeks, but it didn't help, nor did the cool water she gulped from the tap. Her mind wouldn't stop spinning. Was it the house, *him,* his intimidating mother or what? Trying to put the encounter with Louis aside for a moment, she scrutinized the room, searching her memory. *Wasn't this where the old water closet should be?* But then she might be mistaken, it was after all such a very long time ago, and now, after the unexpected encounter with Louis, she was in such a dither that never mind thinking straight, she could barely think at all.

When Tatiana eventually reappeared Louis escorted her to the kitchen. On entering she looked expectantly around, but impressive as it was, she had no recall of having been there before. The only original features, she figured, would be the vaulted ceiling, black from years of smoke escaping from the open hearth where a fire now blazed, the barred windows and the flagstone floor. The rest of the room was fitted with all the apparatus of a modern kitchen. She was still musing when her thoughts were interrupted by Madame Lafont making formal introductions.

'Louis, I want you to meet our guests…'

As Louis was introduced to everyone, Tatiana noticed how, like his father, he kissed her mum's hand and gave a nod of the head as he shook hands with her grandfather and Marcus. Intrigued and totally captivated, she was gazing at him with ill-disguised admiration when he turned, took her hand and raising it to his lips, murmured, '*Enchanté*.'

'I hope you don't mind eating in here, it's so draughty in the dining room at this time of year,' said their hostess.

'Not that we use that part of the chateau much anyway,' added Monsieur Lafont.

Once the formalities were over and everyone, helped by a glass of wine, relaxed, the meal became one of storytelling and laughter.

'We were wondering if the chateau has any ghosts?' said Tatiana, looking pointedly at Marcus.

'Some people say they've seen things, but I never have,' said Monsieur Lafont.

'What sort of *things*?'

'Well the library door's supposed to open by itself, and—'

'Some people say they've heard a woman crying,' said Louis, who'd noticed Marcus and Tatiana's exchange of excited glances.

'I could be showing you—'

'Don't believe it, it's all nonsense, ghosts are nothing but scare stories,' said Madame Lafont, in a terse voice. 'Anyway, there's no scientific proof, none at all.'

'I agree,' said her mum.

'I didn't believe in such things, but I'm no longer quite so certain,' remarked her grandfather. 'I think maybe…'

Her mum frowned at her father. 'Since when?' she demanded. 'Only yesterday you were adamant they didn't exist.'

'Things happen, things change,' he said, airily addressing the wall somewhere above Tatiana's head.

After lunch Madame Lafont insisted on taking them all on a conducted tour of the chateau. That didn't suit Tatiana's plan at all. This was their only opportunity to find Isabella and there wasn't a chance of doing that unless she and Marcus could explore alone. In panic, she turned to Louis, who seeing the desperation in her eyes, volunteered to take them himself, but his mother vetoed his suggestion, saying if there was time he could show them the gardens later.

They progressed slowly from room to room with Madame Lafont recounting the history of the place in minute detail. She explained how after the Revolution ended, a cousin of Philippe Lafont's had returned from exile in Italy and reclaimed the chateau. It had been derelict, home only to birds and rats, with the few remaining contents smashed or burnt.

'So you see it isn't at all how it was in the old days,' she was saying, as they entered an oval salon on the ground floor. She opened the shutters covering the French windows, allowing light to flood the sparsely furnished room. 'And none of the furniture or pictures survived the looting and burning…'

As Madame Lafont droned on, Tatiana was hit by a strange buzzing sensation. 'But surely that's the original piano,' she blurted out, pointing to the far side of the room to what looked like an oblong table with six slender legs.

'It is possible,' said Madam Lafont, running a glacial eye over Tatiana. 'It was in the stables and in such a bad state when we came here that we believe it could be the original, although we can't be sure.'

'It doesn't look much like a piano to me,' said Marcus.

Tatiana stared at the piano, her eyes narrowing. 'You lift the front edge to get at the keys, then fold back the top to reveal the strings,' she said.

'*You can't possibly recognise* it,' said Madame Lafont, in a dismissive tone.

'But I do,' she said, hanging her head. Then looking defiantly at their hostess, added, 'I remember it well.'

'Tatiana!' her mum exclaimed sharply. '*Don't be ridiculous.*'

'Sorry,' she stammered. Everyone's eyes were burning into her, including Marcus's. She held her breath. She wasn't sorry and she wasn't going to give in because for no logical reason, she knew she was right. With her fingers firmly crossed, she closed her eyes for a couple of seconds, then opening them said, 'See if the fifth key from the left, a C, I think, is broken … the ivory should be marked.'

They all crowded around the piano and sure enough the key she'd mentioned had signs of having been repaired. For a moment there was an uncomfortable silence while everyone stared at her, all except Marcus who was watching the curious expression on Louis's face as he gazed at Tatiana, who in turn was looking at the floor trying to suppress her mounting elation.

'How did you know that?'

'Because I was there soon after it was broken,' she said, without thinking.

'But you've never been here before!' exclaimed Monsieur Lafont, scratching what was left of his balding hair.

Marcus nudged Tatiana in the back. 'I expect you dreamt it.'

'Yes, that's it,' she said, albeit reluctantly.

'You and your dreams!' murmured her grandfather. 'Anyway you were right about the key even if you have never seen it before.'

As the tour continued Tatiana knew with increasing certainty that she'd 'come home.' The butterflies in her tummy continued to flutter as more distant memories came flooding back, but she no longer felt sick; not since the Lisette part of her was back where she once belonged. Now all she had to do was to find her *then* mother, Isabella. As they processed through the long gallery with its highly polished floor, Tatiana longed to run and slide on it as she had centuries ago, but with so many people present, managed to resist the urge. Next they came to the room she'd been itching to see, Isabella's boudoir. The room had changed little from how she remembered it in the dream; the walls were still hung with sombre tapestries, and the bed was in the same place, only nowadays it was surrounded by a snaking red rope attached to brass poles to stop tourists sitting on it. Tatiana motioned to Marcus that this was the room, and that somehow they had to engineer to be left alone there.

'Isn't there a secret door in the panelling behind the tapestry?' she asked Louis in a hushed voice. 'Leading to a staircase?'

Louis's eyebrows shot up. 'Why yes! But it isn't a secret; it's just that the tapestry is too long. Come, I'll show you,' he said, taking her arm.

'No, later,' she whispered. '*Sans les parents.*'

Almost another hour passed before the tour was finally over. The adults returned to the fire in the library, leaving Louis to show Marcus and Tatiana the gardens.

Chapter 12

Labyrinth

Marcus, Tatiana and Louis collected their coats and set off along a slate passage to a side-door that opened onto the terrace at the back of the house. *More or less how it looked in my dream,* Tatiana thought, noting a pair of benches and the vine-covered balustrade. They were discussing where to go first when three peacocks came strutting towards them.

Marcus grabbed Tatiana's arm. '*Tati,* look out!'

She turned to Louis and said in as casual voice as she could muster, 'You still have peacocks then?'

'Of course.'

'Don't you mind?'

Louis laughed. 'Why should I be minding? They've always been here.'

'Tati doesn't like the noise they make,' said Marcus. 'It scares her.'

Tatiana's head shot up, her cheeks flushing. 'No it doesn't!'

'Well it certainly used to!' he said, his jaw muscles visibly tightening beneath the skin.

'It is going through my head also,' said Louis, smiling sympathetically at Tatiana. 'Sometimes one is sleeping on my windowsill and it screams, waking me up with a fright; *zut alors, c'est terrible!*'

'It's just such a *horrible* noise,' said Tatiana, suppressing a shudder. 'But I'm not bothered by it anymore.'

'*Bon*. Now, would you like to be seeing the stables and courtyard, or *les jardins*?' asked Louis.

'Both,' said Marcus.

'I wonder, is there a maze?'

'*Mais oui,*' said Louis. 'It's a big tourist attraction. You are wanting to see it?'

'*Absolument, I have* to,' said Tatiana.

'Then we'd better be going there first.'

They walked along the wide terrace, Louis and Marcus together, which suited Tatiana who'd been longing to have time alone to reacquaint herself with her surroundings, all so familiar in a distant sort of way. She'd thought she might be nervous, being back in this place so full of old memories, but surprisingly she wasn't. In fact for no logical reason she was so inexplicably elated that had she been alone she'd probably have danced her way along the terrace, singing. As it was she followed the boys with nothing more than a bounce in her step and a smile playing on her face as she contemplated Louis's back-view. She noticed that although their heads were bent close together and they were laughing as they chatted in a mixture of quaint English and excruciating French, Marcus seemed somewhat stiff, almost restrained.

Tatiana caught up with them by the steps leading to the gardens below, and as Louis hurried them along a tree-lined walk, Marcus mentioned Tatiana's maze dream.

'*This labyrinth?* Or, I think you are calling it a maze, *n'est-ce pas?*'

'Yes. W*as* it this maze, Tati?'

'Can't tell till I've seen it.'

'If it is so, you will be knowing how to reach the middle,' said Louis, with a playful grin, 'and how to free yourself from its serpent-like coils.

'*Oh no*!' she cried, coming to an abrupt halt. 'In the dream, I could do neither – it was a bit of a nightmare really,' she said, averting her gaze in case she started blushing again.

'A nightmare, what is this?' Louis asked.

'*Un cauchemar*,' she explained.

He nodded. 'I hope you won't be finding the real one so terrible.'

As they continued walking Tatiana began to remember the path they were following and knew that at any second it would open out to a long vista of symmetrical flowerbeds and rectangular ornamental ponds flanked by clipped yews. They arrived at the labyrinth as the wintery sun began to sink beneath the tree line, casting deep purple shadows between the tightly clipped hedges. Tatiana knew at once that she was back where she'd been in her dream and, as if on cue, a peacock screamed. *Eeeooowwww, eeeooowwww.* And although it startled her, she didn't utter a sound. There was no need, not since she'd realised it was Lisette's fear, not hers. Once she'd recovered her equilibrium, she let out such a drawn-out sigh that Louis placed a hand on her shoulder and inquired if she was all right.

'*Ça va?*'

'*Oui absolument,* I'm...' she was saying, when she spotted the glowering expression on Marcus's face.

'Aren't we going in?' asked Marcus in an irritated voice.

'Do you want to be going alone?'

'You bet,' said Marcus. Without so much as a backward glance at Louis or Tatiana, he turned on his heel and went striding towards the entrance. Tatiana deliberated for a moment. *Marcus seemed upset, what had she done*? She was starting after him when Louis put out a restraining hand.

'Let him go, give him time before you *commence*.'

The tone of his voice made Tatiana glance quizzically at Louis, who caught her gaze. The intense look in his eyes set her head spinning, and blanching, she turned away. *What was it about him?*

'Yes, much better to let Marcus explore on his own,' she said, giving Louis a quick uncertain smile. *Give him time to get over whatever was bugging him.*

Tatiana stood at the entrance to the maze with a sense of foreboding. She couldn't help but remember how hopelessly lost she'd been in her dream. 'Is it *very* difficult to find the middle?'

she asked.

'*Mais oui,* it's easy to lose yourself, but all labyrinths have a system and once you are knowing it, then it's simple. After you've tried, I'll explain how it's working.'

While Louis and Tatiana, oblivious of time and the lowering sun, chatted away, Marcus was sprinting up and down the narrow passages between the hedges. He ran from one junction to the next, randomly turning left or right until flying around a corner he unexpectedly found himself in the middle.

Tatiana entered the maze at a sedate walk, methodically attempting to work out which way to turn each time she was confronted by a choice. But as the light fell to an ominous gloom, she quickened her pace and began to run. After a series of frustrating dead-ends and wrong turns, she finally made it to the centre, and was catching her breath when she saw a small boy waving at her from behind a vast sarcophagus.

Surprised, she hesitated; but then as she waved back, he grinned and disappeared.

'Wait!' she shouted. '*Qui est toi*?' She darted around the sarcophagus only to find he'd vanished. 'Oh no! Not another one,' she muttered.

Tatiana wandered slowly round the circle. She knew there was little hope of the boy reappearing if he was a ghost, for as she'd recently discovered, earth-bound spirits were so elusive that they never appeared for more than a few seconds in daylight. She fingered the box containing Isabella's hair, hoping it might get her to materialise, but nothing more untoward happened.

'It's so frustrating!' she cried. 'How can we possibly help if you remain so elusive?'

She'd scarcely finished her mutterings when she registered the sarcophagus. Her breath quickened as she ran her hands over the polished marble. *Could Isabella's bones be here, not in Paris after all?* She was pondering this new possibility when she felt a rush of air and looking up, saw a pair of peacocks flying off to roost for the night. No longer fazed, she watched till they were out of sight, then, realising it was almost dark, headed to where she'd seen a feather flutter to the ground, stooped to pick it up and twiddling it between her fingers, set off. The interior of the maze was now in near darkness and as her steps faltered, she couldn't help wishing she'd left a trail like Ariadne to show her the way out. *Ariadne! The labyrinth! Was this the place Natasha was referring to in her notebooks, not the Catacombs? Had she seen Isabella here?*

'Tatiana! Bravo! You've made it – I was thinking I would have to be seeking you out,' said Louis, making Tatiana smile. 'Were you reaching the middle?'

'Yes, although at one point I thought I'd never get there and be lost forever like in my dream; when unexpectedly and without really trying, I was there... Did either of you see a little boy go in?'

'No. Did you see one?' asked Marcus.

'I thought so, but then, maybe not, just a trick of the light I expect,' she said, biting her lip.

'*Non*, Tatiana, it will be one of the farmer's boys; they often are playing here.'

'Pity, I thought ... well it doesn't matter.'

Marcus nudged her. 'Don't tell me he didn't have any front teeth.'

Tatiana flinched. 'Marcus! You're right, he didn't,' she whispered. 'Do you think it's just coincidence or '*him*' following me?'

'Don't know, but hey! You found one too,' exclaimed Marcus, pointing at Tatiana's feather.

'*Et moi aussi*!' said Louis. 'I also am finding one, they will have fallen from the birds.'

'So you have *white* peacocks,' Marcus said, sounding disappointed by such a mundane explanation for what, could have been a potent omen.

'Well *non*,' said Louis, looking surprised, 'ours are blue, but many years ago there were only white birds here, the mistress at the time preferred them as they would complement whatever she was wearing, or so the *histoire* says.'

'Imagine having animals to match your clothes!' said Tatiana. 'When was that?'

'Before the Revolution,' said Louis. 'No one would have survived such *vanité* during the Commune.'

'If there aren't any white peacocks, then where did these come from?' asked Marcus.

'Passing angels?' said Tatiana, twirling around flapping her arms up and down. 'Do you suppose the lady in question could have been Isabella?'

'*Peut-être,* you'll have to ask *Maman*.'

Marcus and Louis looked at the feathers, the ecstatic expression on Tatiana's face, and burst out laughing. Tatiana, relieved that the boys seemed to have got over their initial hostilities, couldn't help but join in.

'Dropped by a spirit you are thinking, *non*?' asked Louis.

'A ghost!' yelped Tatiana, cheerfully pretending she hadn't had exactly the same thought.

'Why do you say that?' asked Marcus. 'Has anyone seen ghosts in the maze?'

'Not that I am knowing, but a friend from Scandinavia told me that in her country the old peoples are calling labyrinths "spirit traps", for they believe that the lost souls of people who don't die properly and stay on earth as ghosts only are moving in straight lines and so get caught in the coils of the labyrinth.'

'Interesting,' said Marcus. 'But why would ghosts want to go into a maze?'

'They're supposed to follow living people.'

Tatiana let out an inaudible sigh. 'So the maze could be full of lost souls?'

'Possibly.'

'Well, your mum wouldn't believe that.'

'Certainly not,' he said, laughing. 'But if you're interested in ghosts, I'll show you the rooms that are meant to be haunted, then you can be seeing for yourselves.'

On the way back to the chateau, Marcus and Tatiana made a hasty plan for him to divert Louis so Tatiana could have time alone in the haunted rooms. Their plan worked, but in spite of her having ample time, she didn't get the slightest impression of any lurking spirits. Their explorations over, they returned to the library where Louis's parents were showing Tatiana's mum and Jacques a collection of family papers.

While the others had tea, Marcus and Tatiana looked at the documents spread out on the table. There were letters still bearing the remnants of red wax seals, maps, official papers, account books and a bundle of diaries tied together with faded blue ribbon, which immediately caught Tatiana's eye. She untied the ribbon and opened one of the small leather-bound books. She was so hoping they'd be Henriette's lost diaries, but no such luck for she soon came across references to the Napoleonic wars and knew they were of no real interest to her. Marcus was helping put the documents back in their box when a fragment of blue ribbon, tied in a bow, fell on the floor. He picked it up and held it out to Madam Lafont, who shook her head and pointed towards the fire. He stood before the burning logs fingering the ribbon and was reaching out to toss it into the flames when he changed his mind, and slipped it into his pocket instead.

Later that evening, as Tatiana went to kiss her grandfather goodnight, he took two small plastic bags from the table beside him and handed one to her.

'This is for you,' he said. 'But before you open it I want you all to see what I have here.' He placed the other bag on the table and keeping his eyes fixed on her mum's face, slowly pulled out a pale blue silk tie covered in a pattern of tiny forget-me-nots.

'Voilà!'

'Oh,' cried her mum, '*I don't believe it*! You went to check?'

'*Mais oui.*'

'Tati … I'm so sorry! I shouldn't have shouted at you earlier.'

'My Natasha was right, she *had* taken it to the cleaners and they still had it! *C'est merveilleux*!' he said, clasping Tatiana to his bony old body.

'Now do you believe that she isn't gone for good?'

'*Mais oui,* of course, only she could have known about my tie, so she has to be somewhere, waiting for me,' he said, brushing the back of his hand across his eyes. 'My darling Natasha gave it to me for our anniversary the year she died; she knew she hadn't long to live so we made many special trips and I wore it on every occasion to fill it with happy memories of our last months together.'

'I'm *so glad* you've got it back.'

'And so am I, thanks to you and your "ghosts".'

'*Dream,* Grand-père, it was a dream.'

'So you say, but I prefer to think of her as a ghost, then she can stay here with me! Now for your gift, Tati, your reward for making a sad old man very happy.'

Tatiana peeked into the bag before sliding out a CD. 'Grand-Père, how lovely! "*French Folk Songs*".'

'It has that song you are always humming, so I thought you'd better have it.'

'*My tune*? Does it really?'

'Yes, see, "*La Jeune et Gentille Lisette*".'

'This is brilliant. Thank you so much,' she said, throwing her arms around his scrawny neck and kissing him on both cheeks.

Chapter 13

Of Dreams and Reality

Before going to bed Tatiana showed Marcus some passages she'd transcribed from Natasha's notebooks.

'She doesn't say where the information came from, but it seems Lisette was brought up by Isabella's cousin André and his wife, Henriette, in St Petersburg.'

'So you were right when you said you thought she fancied him. Anything else?'

'Well, come and have a look at these lists I've found – see what you think.'

But Marcus, with his jaw set and his fists balling in his pockets, stayed right where he was. *Uh-oh! What was the matter with him?* She thought he'd been rather quiet and withdrawn since they'd got back, and now he wouldn't even come near her. *Had she upset him?*

'You can't see like that,' she said, making room for him beside her. 'Sit down.' But seemingly determined to remain aloof, he didn't move.

'You okay?' she asked, looking at him through her eyelashes.

'Yup,' he said, his voice flat and morose. 'But you're quite alike you know.'

'Who? Louis and me?'

'Yes. I couldn't help noticing how you two kept chatting in French, all intimate and animated, like old friends. And you have the same formal, old-fashioned manners and way of speaking, particularly to grown-ups. They seemed a bit odd back home, but here, it's different. Here, it's you who's normal, not me,' he said.

So that was it – he'd felt excluded.

'I'm so sorry, but I am half-French and ... I hope you haven't got a problem with him … and me?'

'No, least not with you…'

'Well if you don't like Louis you needn't worry, we're not likely to see him again,' she said, and giving him a bright smile turned back to the notebooks.

'See, under Philippe's name she's written *imprisoned, tribunal, beheaded at Concorde, buried,* so at least *he* must have a grave somewhere! Then below Isabella's name two words, *imprisoned* and *released,* followed by, *cause and date of death unknown.*'

'This is crazy! If Natasha didn't know, how does she expect us to find out?' said Marcus, still sounding rather terse.

'I don't know, but she must have been on to something because in this other notebook she's circled random words that must relate to her. "*Carmes*", which we already know about, then "*green boudoir, check maze on 10th, Infirmière des Smaritiens*" and wait for it, "*Catacombs!*"'

'That's settled then, we're definitely going back tomorrow. She has to be there 'cos it fits with the references to Ariadne *and* they're dark *and below ground* unlike the maze.'

That night, Tatiana had a nightmare about the chateau in which everything was terribly wrong. At first she was trying to get it ready for a visitor, but every room she went into had broken furniture strewn haphazardly about the floor; tables with legs missing were tossed on their sides, seats had been ripped out of chairs, pictures torn from the walls, the canvases slashed, and the curtains lying in crumpled heaps on the floor were soiled with human excrement. Fires, started in the ransacked rooms, had left the walls smoke-streaked and blackened and an acrid smell hung over the charred remains of the family possessions. She noticed the twisted corpse of a sightless cat tossed across a splintered chest, its body pierced through the belly by a shaft of wood. The sheer revulsion of what human beings were capable of doing was too much and she wanted to escape, but found herself unable to leave.

She ran from room to room, clenching and unclenching her fists as she went, until reaching the music room, and there she saw it, the piano. The one where she'd learnt to play the latest popular pieces from Paris, and where she'd once caught André and her mother wrapped in a sensuous embrace. Even from a distance she could see it was damaged. The lid wrenched off, a slop bucket thrown inside, depositing its festering remains amongst the exposed hammers and strings. That was it; she finally snapped, and seizing the bucket, hurled it through the nearest window.

The tinkle of falling glass hitting the floor merged with strains of a melody reviving in her mind. She swept the debris from the keys, a couple were damaged, but otherwise the keyboard was relatively unscathed. For a moment her extended fingers hovered over the keys; then there it was; music, her music, filling the room, echoed notes from a familiar symphony. The sound, still a part of the room, clinging like dust to the curtains, the notes vibrating with flashes of colour in her head; unearthly music, remnants from the carefree, hedonistic days before the Revolution.

She shook her head, bringing her mind back to the task in hand, and resumed her inspection of the chateau before deciding it was no place to bring a sick person. She was picking her way across the long gallery, doing her best to avoid the shards of shattered mirror littering the floor, when her attention was drawn to the spiky patterns reflected on the ceiling and in so doing, caught sight of herself in a jagged fragment still suspended precariously on the wall. '*Who* are you?' she asked, but the only response came from a hooded crow cawing on the window ledge outside.

While Katya took Jacques to his doctor's appointment the following morning, Marcus and Tatiana returned to the

Catacombs to check whether the children had gone.

Once they entered the long dark passage they started to run and although they kept running it was still several minutes before they slid to a halt at the entrance to the ossuary where, deliberately ignoring the sign above the doorway, Tatiana darted into 'The Empire of Death'.

'Where shall we start?' she asked.

'The gallery with the skull pillars,' said Marcus. 'Then you can see if my dream was correct and they're still there.'

Over an hour had passed and they were still in the gallery, waiting. They'd tried telepathy, having mental conversations with the children, but they hadn't appeared.

'They must have gone,' ventured Marcus.

'Let's hope so, but I'll try one last thing before we go.' She knelt, closed her eyes and started singing to *their* tune.

'Are you still here?' she sang,

'If you are, please let us help you.'

'Those aren't the words *they* sang,' protested Marcus.

Tatiana opened her eyes. 'I haven't had time to learn the French ones yet; anyway, it's the tune that matters.'

Doing her best to ignore Marcus's tightly folded arms, Tatiana resumed her singing.

'We've come to help you,

but can't unless you—'

She was still singing when the temperature suddenly plunged and the surrounding air started vibrating. She turned and there, coming towards them, were three misty shadows.

'Marcus, they're here! Beam them light,' she sang.

'How do I do that?'

'Imagine a bright spotlight and ... be mentally strong and "will" them into it.'

'Where'd you get that from, Tati?'

'It just sort of popped into my head,' she said. 'I think Natasha's helping, and we mustn't show any weakness or doubt.

Marcus, we need to get this right, in case we ever find Isabella.'

'Okay, so no problem at all! Like we do this every day of the week! And while we're about it we'll whistle up Isabella and send her off at the same time!'

'*Marcus!* Why so sarcastic?'

Marcus pulled a face and shrugged. 'It's … I just don't know exactly how to use my *will*, and beam light, that's all.'

'I don't either, but we have to try.'

After a few minutes of them focusing all their energy on the children, Tatiana saw the expression on the two girls' faces change from one of puzzled solemnity to broad smiles. Encouraged by the now grinning boy, the girls waved goodbye before melting into the bright light filtering through the bone-filled walls of the ossuary.

'*That's brilliant,* I do believe they've really gone this time,' exclaimed Tatiana. 'It was strange though, because the boy looked like he was helping us, or maybe it was the girls… *Marcus*?'

'What?'

'Can't you feel it?'

'Feel what?'

'That jangling cold,' she said.

'I thought it had just warmed up,' he said, but then as he went to pull her to her feet, she noticed him shiver violently.

'I can't see anything, but suddenly there's this icy sensation running right through me, so there *definitely* has to be something here.

'Something *"other"*, pulsating … in waves. Marcus … let's get out of here.'

Tatiana glanced around, checking for the best way out, when she went rigid. 'Marcus, don't look!'

But her warning was no use. Although Marcus couldn't see anything, he was struck by a terrible, irrational fear, intensified by the look on Tatiana's face. Advancing from every direction through the porous bones came a multitude of the silently whispering dead. They emerged from the shadows, drifting on the cold mist-laden air, gliding towards them, beseeching with hollow, sightless eyes, their transparent bony hands outstretched and pleading.

'Oh … my … God!' hissed Tatiana, shielding her eyes with her arm.

'What is it?'

'There're hundreds of them … everywhere. We've got to get out of here.'

'Let's run for it,' he said.

Tatiana's hands shook as she grabbed Marcus's sleeve. 'We can't. We're … surrounded,' she stuttered. 'Completely hemmed in, there's no way through … unless…' She clenched her jaw. *This was a test – the moment not to be flaky and give in. Of course she could do it, just hadn't needed to before.*

It was then that something she'd seen in a Kung-Fu film flashed into her mind. 'I know what we have to do; we have to let go of our fear. No matter what we feel, this is *very important*; then and only then, can we walk through them, focusing our will by imagining sabres of light, lighting up the darkness surrounding these, these … lost souls. And although I can see them, I know they're not solid, that *we can* walk straight through them. But if we have any doubts we will fail and then heaven knows what will happen. Let's go and whatever happens *show no fear*, that's our only defence.'

'I'm with you, Tati, so *let's smile.*'

'Thanks, but as for *smiling!* Marcus get real!'

'Just do it, Tati.'

Marcus braced his shoulders, turned, and seizing Tatiana's hand strode purposefully towards the advancing phantoms. Tatiana, confronted by the multitude, gulped and momentarily dragged her heels, but Marcus was pulling and there was nothing for it, *she had to go*. Shielding her eyes with her free hand she stopped resisting and allowed Marcus to steer her towards the ghostly forms. As she came face to face with a pair of desperate, unseeing eyes, she unclenched her teeth enough to form her lips into the semblance of a contorted smile, all the while sending out a silent plea of help for the lost souls surrounding them. Neither felt anything other than a powerful tremor convulse their bodies as they passed through the mass of extended hands and transparent bodies. It was as if the phantoms didn't exist.

Once back on the street above the Catacombs, they stood on the pavement under the leaden December sky, clinging to each other and inhaling great gulps of icy air into their lungs to rid themselves of the horror of what lay beneath their feet.

'Bloody hell! What a nightmare!'

'Marcus, shouldn't we have helped them?'

'No way, not possibly, you know that.'

'Do you think they were going to do something terrible to us.'

Marcus thought for a minute. 'I don't know, but I doubt they meant us any harm.'

'Perhaps they were drawn to the light when the children left and wanted help too.'

'Or curiosity, but we're not going back to find out.'

They were making their way back towards the Metro when Tatiana frowned, and turned to Marcus. 'Supposing Isabella was amongst them?'

Marcus shrugged. 'If she was, we couldn't possibly have done anything. And I don't know about you, but I really don't fancy going back.'

'Me neither, but what about her?'

'I think we should try the chateau again, after all, it does seem the most logical place for her to be,' said Marcus.

'I don't know how we'll manage that.'

'The same way Natasha did, we'll go on an open day.'

'But it isn't open at this time of year.'

'Then we'll have to ask your mum…'

Louis's phone call came just as they were sitting down for supper. He told Katya that he was coming to Paris the following day and asked if Tatiana and Marcus might like to join him for lunch at the Louvre.

'It's so kind of Louis,' her mum said, giving them the good news. 'So much healthier to spend the day with him instead of running around searching for tombs and dead relatives.'

Tatiana sighed and said nothing, but a joyous look of anticipation filled her eyes as she realised this was their opportunity to enlist Louis's help, she just had to get back to the chateau.

Chapter 14

Revolutionaries Past and Present

The next morning found Tatiana staring into her wardrobe; she hadn't a clue what to wear. She'd hoped to see Louis again one day, and now with the ice between the families finally broken, it had seemed likely that they would, but she hadn't dared hope it would be quite so soon. Everything she put on seemed wrong and by the time her mum came to see what she was doing, her room looked like the aftermath of a burglary. When she was finally satisfied with her look, she sneaked into her mum's room. She knew her dad would never approve, but she didn't care, he wasn't here and besides, all her friends wore make-up. She rummaged in her mum's make-up bag, found what she needed and left.

They'd arranged to meet in the main entrance of the *Musée du Louvre,* beneath the glass pyramid, and were approaching the rendezvous when Tatiana caught her breath; she'd seen Louis. Oh boy, was she glad she'd settled on skinny jeans tucked into her new black boots with a cashmere polo neck, given to her by Jacques for Christmas. Louis was leaning against a postcard stand, his long white fingers leafing through an art book, and hadn't noticed their arrival, allowing Tatiana time to pause and reacquaint herself with his strong aquiline profile and slightly wavy, dark hair.

'You'll never believe this, Marcus,' she said, 'but I've just remembered something, I'm sure it was Louis I saw in that flashback by the obelisk!'

'Before you'd actually met him?'

'Yes. Not as he is now, but—' She stopped, looking all misty-eyed.

'Tati! Don't tell me…'

'I think I've known him for ever and ever,' she sighed.

'Then you probably have,' said Marcus, in a clipped tone.

'Tatiana! Comme tu est très belle aujourd'hui,' Louis said, taking her by the shoulders and kissing her on both cheeks. Tatiana heard Marcus let out a derisive snort and tried not to squirm as he shoved his hands in his pockets away from Louis's extended one. *Okay, so shaking hands with someone his own age wasn't Marcus's thing, it wasn't hers either, but he'd done it before at the chateau, so why was he being rude now?* She was glaring at him when he sheepishly proffered a hand to Louis.

With the initial awkwardness over, Louis suggested that before going around the museum, they first had lunch. 'I don't know about you, but my stomach is filled with a great hunger.'

During a leisurely meal in one of the museum's many restaurants, they discussed which galleries they should visit.

'Where shall we start, Louis?'

'This, depends on what you are wishing to see. Myself, I want to compare the sarcophagi here with the one at home,' he said.

'I wouldn't mind seeing them, either,' said Marcus.

As Marcus and Louis, who'd hardly exchanged two words during lunch, started discussing the whys and wherefores of sarcophagi, Tatiana saw her opportunity to escape.

'Why don't you go together?' she suggested, but even as she spoke, she could see by Marcus's darkening face and the way Louis turned abruptly away, that this was a bad idea. 'Or we could all go our separate ways and meet up later,' she added brightly. 'Anyway, I'm going to look for that amazing painting of the Revolution by Delacroix.'

'Then we shall *rendezvous* back here in one hour,' said Louis.

Tatiana watched the boys go off then turned in the opposite direction. She wanted time alone. She wandered from room to room, studying the diverse collection of eighteenth-century artefacts and furniture including the gruesome picture of Marat, murdered in the bath. Having found Delacroix's enormous Revolutionary painting of 'Liberty' leading the people, she was lost in contemplation of the bare-breasted woman triumphantly waving the tri-colour flag from the top of a pile of dead bodies, when a hand squeezed her shoulder.

'Marvellous, *n'est-ce pas*?'

'Louis! You startled me,' she said, flushing as he beamed down at her.

'You were lost in thought – *non*?'

'Yes, I can't help feeling, that maybe I lived then.'

Louis inclined his head slightly and Tatiana could see him puzzling over what she'd said. 'In the eighteenth century?'

Not sure what Louis's reaction would be, Tatiana just nodded.

'You are so young, yet saying such funny, interesting things,' he said, with an ill-disguised hint of amusement. 'So you think we've all lived before?'

'Why not, it makes sense to me.'

'Reincarnation?'

'Yes, what about you?'

'Well I would like to think so, *mais,* but…' He shrugged.

'Don't you sometimes feel you've been somewhere before when you haven't, or you already know someone, when you've only just met?' she asked, looking into his eyes.

He tilted his head further, studying her expression. 'Yes, I have been feeling all of those things, like when you were coming to lunch, I was thinking I was knowing you then,' he said, his voice softening.

'Me too.'

'*Vraiment?* Really? I'm so glad, I thought I was being stupid,' he said, with a wry smile.

'I knew you and the house at once, and Marcus said the chateau felt familiar to him too.'

'What did I say?' asked Marcus, joining them by Delacroix's picture.

'We were talking about reincarnation,' explained Tatiana.

'So you're saying we have many lives?'

'I don't *really* know, Louis,' said Tatiana, averting her eyes from his enquiring gaze. 'But suppose we get to choose who we reincarnate with, like our parents and friends, wouldn't that be amazing? That way we'd get to meet up with – special people – like, you know, on-going relationships,' she said, blushing.

Raising one quizzical eyebrow, Louis continued studying Tatiana's face.

'*Vraiment?* You really think it's like that?' he asked, frowning.

'Why not?'

'I need to be thinking about it.' Then, changing to a less serious mode, he looked at Tatiana. 'I am thinking this was you!' he said, pointing to a statue of a scantily clothed dancing girl, causing her to flush the colour of the setting sun, yet again.

'And what about this?' asked Marcus, stopping in front of a picture of a young boy being led to the guillotine.

'Terrible!' said Louis, shaking his head. 'Thousands of people, young, old, even innocent children were executed, for what exactly? There was no trust anywhere, not even within families. The Revolution is so often being idealised when for most people it was not a good time to be living in France.' He looked hard at Tatiana.

The strength of feeling in Louis's voice made Tatiana flinch and wonder if she was being rebuked for her earlier remark or if it was more than that. For a second the images she'd seen by the obelisk came flooding back and for a wild moment she saw Louis as the Chevalier saving her family from execution, but then realised he would undoubtedly reject such a silly idea as romantic nonsense.

They left the Louvre and were sauntering towards the Metro when the crowd separated Marcus and Tatiana from Louis, giving them time for a hurried discussion about enlisting his help in finding Isabella. Tatiana's dream from the night before seemed to throw doubt on her having died in Paris and Louis's remark about labyrinths trapping spirits, coupled with the white feathers and the boy, made her wonder if Isabella could be in the sarcophagus.

'Ask him while I wait here,' urged Marcus.

Tatiana felt awkward asking such a favour and kept looking at the ground, shrugging and gesticulating, but when Louis took out his mobile and started punching in numbers, she turned, thumbs up and beckoned to Marcus.

'Any luck?' he asked, while Louis was busy on the phone.

'Well he was really interested about Isabella, and although the idea of rescuing a ghost was quite beyond him, he said he'd try and arrange for us to go back to the chateau. He's ringing his mum now.'

'I can't imagine how his parents will react to that.'

'I only suggested the maze to Louis.'

'Why? Hardly likely she'd have died in the maze.'

'Somehow it sounded less demanding. Anyway, I started by asking him if *he* could see if she was there ... and send her away for us.'

'But he couldn't do that...'

'I know, that's why I suggested it, so he'd *have* to ask *us*!'

'Tati!'

'It's all fixed,' said Louis, pocketing his phone. 'Tomorrow, if it's okay with you. She's going to ring your maman, Tatiana.'

'That's brilliant, thank you so much,' she said, smiling.

'Till tomorrow then,' said Louis. He brushed Tatiana's cheek with his lips, and with a nod to Marcus, set off for the Metro.

'He does such strange things,' said Marcus, glaring at Louis's departing figure.

'He's just *wonderfully* French,' she said, pressing a hand to her cheek. Then realising that Marcus was probably irritated by Louis's sophistication, added rather lamely, 'Anyway Mum thinks he has beautiful manners.'

'Unlike me,' he muttered.

'I didn't say that, you just don't like him,' she said, scowling.

'It's not that, it's just all this talking in French so I can't understand, and he's so … foreign, like you are sometimes.'

'Are you saying you don't…?'

'No, of course not, you're the best,' he said. And wrinkling his nose, said with his usual honesty, 'I just … don't like the way he keeps kissing you.'

Tatiana's mum was adamant; she was not going to take them. Firstly she had to drive her father to an appointment and secondly she said it was quite out of the question to impose themselves on their relatives again after such a short acquaintance, besides they'd only just been there.

Tatiana turned to her grandfather for support, but he agreed with her mum.

'*Mais non*! You've had lunch with Louis today, and really we should return their hospitality before even thinking of going back, it's only polite.'

'Why's everyone so formal in France?' grumbled Marcus.

When the phone eventually went, Tatiana was plunged into despair as she heard her mum thanking Madam Lafont profusely, but declining the invitation, saying she didn't want them being a nuisance and bothering poor Louis.

'Oh *please,* Mum, can't we?'

'Absolutely not, Tatiana, I haven't the time to drive you, besides she told me they'd be out for the day so it's quite out of the question.'

'But *we have to*!'

'Nonsense, of course you don't.'

'Can't we, please, Grand-pére?'

Her grandfather pursed his lips into a thin, tight line, hesitated, and then shook his head. '*Non, absolument pas, et voilà tout*!'

Tatiana stood up and in a clipped tone said good night before stomping off to text Louis from her room. She fingered her phone, what was she going to say? She had to go; the chateau was her only hope, but how? She was tossing her phone from hand to hand when she looked up to see Marcus hovering in the passage outside her room.

'You okay, Tati?'

'I suppose so, but Mum's so annoying, and just when things were looking more positive,' she said, clenching her jaw.

In a bound Marcus was across the room hugging her. 'She doesn't mean to be difficult, she just doesn't understand,' he said. 'Don't worry, we'll think of something.'

'Well, I don't know what exactly.'

The next day Marcus and Tatiana set off to spend the day at the Eiffel Tower. On the journey there Marcus took the opportunity of studying the guidebook, and was still reading when the Metro stopped at the mainline station of Montparnasse, where Tatiana stood up.

'Do we change here?'

'Yes,' she said, airily, 'to a proper train.'

'*A train,* where to?'

'Where do you think? We're going to Clèrmency.'

Marcus grabbed Tatiana's arm. '*We can't,* your mum will go ballistic; you know she will.'

Tatiana didn't answer, couldn't because she knew he was right, but that wasn't going to stop her, she had to go. She shook herself free and ran towards the ticket office, Marcus keeping pace beside her.

'Tati, we can't!'

'We *can,*' she said, rounding on him. 'Don't you see, I *have* to go. We're getting nowhere, time's running out and we go back to England in a few days. If we don't find her, I'll have let Natasha down and '*it*' will go on plaguing me, sending me crazy,' she shouted. 'And if you're not up for it, I'm going on my own.'

Marcus stopped, and raising his hands in the air, said, 'Okay, calm down, I'm coming with you.'

After a moment's wavering, she reached up and kissed his cheek. 'Thanks, Marcus, you're a star, and don't worry about Mum, we'll be back long before dark, so she'll never know.' But as she spoke her gaze came to rest on the station clock and a sense of foreboding came over her. 'Well, we should be.'

Chapter 15

Blizzard and Blackout

When they arrived at Clèrmency station, Louis was there, waiting for them in an ancient red and white striped Deux Chevaux. One look at him and Tatiana found herself in a dizzying fluster of uncertain excitement. A feeling that intensified as he took her by the shoulders and slowly kissed her on both cheeks. But as Louis released her, she noticed Marcus's clenched jaw and sullen expression.

'Brilliant car, don't you think, Marcus?' she said, trying to diffuse what she could see developing into a thoroughly awkward situation. She couldn't risk Marcus becoming bolshie, not now they'd got here.

'Yeah. Like *seriously* different,' he finally conceded. And it was; with its bold stripes and roll-down canvas top, it was quite unlike any car either of them had ever seen before.

'*C'est bon, n'est-ce pas?* Father bought it for me to learn driving on. I've only just taken my test, so I shouldn't be—'

'We're not bothered by that,' said Tatiana, scrambling into the back seat. '*We* shouldn't even be here.'

'My parents won't be back till later, so apart from Marie, who'll be going home before lunch, we'll have the place to ourselves.'

'I've been thinking Isabella might be in the sarcophagus,' said Marcus.

'*C'est possible,*' said Louis, shaking his head, 'but unlikely, since the Egyptian things weren't coming to France until after Napoleon's first expedition to Egypt in 1798.'

Once at the chateau, Louis said that since he didn't understand exactly what they wanted to do, they might like to be left to do their own thing. Marcus and Tatiana readily agreed. They'd already decided their first priority was to make another thorough search of the building, just in case Louis's parents returned early, and this time to concentrate on the rooms she'd seen in her dreams.

Tatiana went straight upstairs and through the mirrored gallery to what she remembered as Isabella's bedroom. Tiptoeing, as if afraid of disturbing any unseen inhabitants, she inspected every aspect of the room, including the secret door behind the tapestry. She ran her hands over the faded velvet curtains, perched on a gilt edged chair and admired the remnants of Chinese wallpaper, but knowing that little other than possibly the bed were from Isabella's days, they were of no real interest to her. While waiting for something to happen, she ducked under the red ropes, used to keep tourists at bay, and climbed onto the ornate four-poster bed. There she stretched out; her long hair fanned over the silk covers and clutching the box containing Isabella's hair to her chest, closed her eyes.

'Come and haunt me,' she pleaded. 'I need to see you … *please.*'

She remained alert, conscious of the steady beat of her heart, but nothing else. And so the silence remained, taut and unbroken until faint creaks from the panelling and an almost imperceptible rustle of wind catching in the casement windows, made her stiffen. She lay motionless, expectant yet apprehensive, as the chill of the unheated room seeped into her bones. Even the watery sun slanting through the long windows made no difference to the cold. She wrapped her arms around herself and opening her eyes, saw her breath billowing in puffs of grey vapour in the icy air above her head.

'Why won't you come?' she whispered. 'I only want to help … I have to, I've promised.' Determined not to be defeated, she closed her eyes and started a rhythmic, mind-clearing breathing exercise, repeating it over and over again, until, yes! *What was that? Those were definitely voices, several of them, and footsteps … and the unmistakable school locker room smell of un-washed bodies. Only this was no school locker room, far from it; she'd slipped away from the twenty-first century, and returned to her life as Lisette.*

Lisette had positioned herself on an upholstered window seat, half-hidden by the looped-back curtains; from here she could observe her parents' guests, whilst seemingly engrossed in a book.

There had been many people gathered at the chateau over the last few days and the usually dim passages blazed with dozens of dripping candles, the wax building into increasingly tall and rugged stalagmites in intervals along the parquet floor. These structures, she'd noticed, were providing a new and interesting place for the milling dogs to cock their legs. Two elegant ladies dressed in the latest Paris fashion with wide, pannier skirts and towering wigs, teetered past, holding perfumed kerchiefs to their noses. Lisette glanced up, but they were so engrossed in their exchange of salacious gossip, that they were unaware of either her, or of their silken skirts brushing through a trail of dog pee. *If only Cécile wasn't so busy flirting with the guests and would sit with her, tell her about the scandals at court, or better still—*

'May I enquire what is it that so occupies you, *Mademoiselle?*'

Lisette jumped to her feet and blushing, bobbed a curtsy. *How could she have not heard the Chevalier approaching, him of all people?* 'Why it's … Voltaire,' she said, hiding the book behind her back, only to see Henri Pellerin's eyebrows shoot up.

'Voltaire indeed! So you like philosophy,' he said, and with a wave of the hand, suggested they should sit. Lisette hardly dared breathe. *Henri, actually sitting, talking with her!* She hastily gathered in the folds of her skirts to make room for him in the confined space. He was pressed so close she could smell the pomade on his hair and see every stitch of the fine embroidery edging his frockcoat, and how her heart danced.

'And have you also read the works of that other great man of enlightened thought, Rousseau?'

'I have, only it was a novel, not one of his serious works,' she said, blushing. 'Please, monsieur, I beg you, do not tell my maman for she would not approve.'

The Chevalier, turned to face Lisette and, as if seeing her for the first time, took her hand, raised it to his lips and smiled. 'Your secret is safe with me, and thank you for the warning. I also like to read works by those great men and would be very interested to have your opinion.'

It wasn't until after the guests had left and her father's coach was being made ready for his departure to Paris, accompanied by the dashing Chevalier, that she fully understood why her maman was to remain in the country.

'If Paris is becoming so dangerous, Henriette, why is Cécile allowed to return. Is it because of the Chevalier?'

'No. Cécile insisted on going in order to persuade her aunt to leave, for it seems her aunt was quite refusing to go, saying she was perfectly safe from the agitators at Versailles, and that it would be far too dull for her to be buried away in the country.'

'Better to be bored than dead,' Lisette said, raising her voice over the shrieking of a peacock outside.

'Shh. You mustn't say such things, besides if André's to be believed, it may not be quite as safe in the country as everyone likes to believe.'

As the warmth of the eighteenth-century summer, together with its sounds and smells receded, the wintery chill brought Tatiana back to her senses. She opened her eyes, staring vacantly at the bed canopy. *No wonder Lisette was infatuated by Henri, she could really fancy him herself.* She'd have liked to stay there daydreaming but knew she didn't have time. *How peculiar seeing all those other people and not Isabella? Why? She must have been there, or was she too preoccupied with her guests to bother herself with her daughter.* With a confused shake of her head she sat up, and convinced she'd freeze to death if she stayed any longer, slid off the bed and was heading for the room of the weeping woman when she spotted Marcus at the far end of the mirrored gallery.

'Any luck?' she called.

'No, what about you?'

'Nothing, but I haven't tried the haunted room yet, I was leaving it till last.'

'I'll meet you there then.'

The supposedly haunted room faced north and seemed particularly dark after the sunny gallery. As they stood in the room the sombre tapestries covering the walls combined with dark oak furniture only served to make it appear even gloomier than it was. Tatiana shivered, stamped her feet and zipped her coat up to her neck.

'Let's be quick, it's freezing in here.'

'You try telling a ghost to be quick!' he said, rolling his eyes.

'Feel anything?'

'No, but I think we should sit down and see what happens.'

Tatiana sat, hugging herself against the cold, on one of the hard upright chairs placed around the wall. She started by willing something, anything to happen, but she was finding it difficult to switch off, her mind kept wandering. She knew exactly what was bothering her, Louis. She just couldn't stop thinking about him, or the Chevalier. There was something indefinable, a dizzying sense of desperation that swelled within her at the thought of possibly never seeing him again, of losing him! *Yet she hardly knew him, so how silly was that?* And then her thoughts turned to Marcus. He was a true and loyal friend, the only person who'd ever come close to understanding her. *But this wasn't the time to dwell on boys, she had to focus on Isabella.*

They'd been sitting very still on the hard upright chairs for ages, when Tatiana, unable to stand it anymore, peered through half-closed lids at Marcus and seeing his chill-pinched face, jumped to her feet. 'This is hopeless, if it was Isabella people heard crying, she's certainly not crying now.'

'Good, I'm glad you've decided that. I'm so cold I can't think of anything except hot food, and maybe you,' said Marcus, grinning. 'Only not in that order.'

Tatiana's mouth twitched trying not to laugh. 'Food I think. Louis said something about lunch in the kitchen.'

'Let's go then', said Marcus heading for the door.

After they'd devoured bowls of steaming beetroot soup with crusty olive bread, followed by a quiche, left for them by Marie, they felt a lot more cheerful in spite of the unproductive morning.

'So nothing,' groaned Marcus.

'But we still have the maze and personally, I bet that's where she is,' said Tatiana, still doggedly determined to remain positive.

'You should visit it soon,' said Louis, looking at his watch. 'Your train leaves in three hours.'

Tatiana jumped up and passing the window noticed the sky had become ominously overcast with a yellowish tinge. 'We must go to the maze, *now,* Marcus before it rains.'

They'd hardly reached the end of the terrace when it started to snow. Not much, just a few big fat flakes like feathers shaken from a pillow, floating on the still air.

'What shall we do?'

'Keep going, it's not that far,' said Marcus, striding on. But the snow kept falling, thicker and faster until they couldn't see.

'Marcus! Tatiana!' They heard, and turning saw the blurred shape of Louis coming towards them.

'This is not good, you will have to be waiting until it stops,' he said, hurrying them back to the chateau.

'We haven't time to wait,' said Marcus.

'Well, it wasn't forecasting snow, so it stops soon.'

Tatiana stared at Louis. 'No, I don't think so,' she said, her eyes taking on a faraway look.

But it didn't stop. It became worse and worse and the wind got up driving the snow into ever deepening drifts. Once or twice they left the warmth of the kitchen fire to look outside, only to find no change and so the minutes ticked agonisingly by until it was time to leave for the station. Tatiana couldn't bear it; they couldn't leave, they hadn't completed their mission and there now seemed little hope they would. All the horrors would start again, she just knew it, and as if to confirm her fears, the dreaded icy-finger sensation started jabbing inside her again.

They hurried out to where the car was parked in front of the chateau.

'It's not possible to be moving the car from here,' said Louis, scrunching over the white carpet that blanketed everything outside including his car. 'Even with chains we won't be getting through the drifts.'

'You mean we *can't* go?' asked Marcus.

'No, you have to stay, for days maybe!'

Yay!' yelled Marcus, and grinning, punched the air.

Tatiana's face lit up, her hunch at the station was right. *How brilliant was that?* She scooped-up a handful of the lifesaving snow and licked it, *yum, delicious as lemon sorbet – only better – it had given them more time.* Then a horrifying thought struck, clouding her face, and making her heart sink. *Mum! Now she really was in trouble. She'd know she'd lied. There could be no hiding where they were now.*

'Tati!'

'*Marcus*!' shrieked Tatiana, as his missile knocked her out of her troubled reverie. Then as another snowball, lobbed by Louis, hit her hard on the back, she scrambled into action and started retaliating.

It was some time later, whilst stamping the snow off their shoes by the side door, that they heard the telephone ringing. It was Louis's parents calling to say they were snowbound and unable to get back. But that wasn't the end of it, because they heard him trying to reassure his mum he'd be all right on his own, and then it seemed he was having to put up a fight to stop her arranging for Marie to sleep in. Finally, looking really exasperated, he hung up.

'Maman! She's always so anxious about me, the way she behaves, you would be thinking I was still eight not nearly eighteen.'

Tatiana nodded sympathetically; she knew just what it was like. 'Oh no! Mum! I'd better ring her; she'll be really flapping by now. I don't suppose you'd like to call her for me, would you, Louis?' she said, chewing her lip.

Louis raised an eyebrow. 'Does she know you're here?'

Tatiana shuffled her feet and stared at the floor. 'No. She thinks we're at the Eiffel Tower.'

'No problem, I'll explain,' he said. Then grinning at her impudence, added, 'I'll tell her I was insisting.'

No sooner had he spoken than Tatiana's mobile started ringing. 'No! I don't believe it,' she said, blanching, 'it's Dad!'

Tatiana was so subdued and distracted whilst cooking the pasta for their supper, that she splattered her pale pink jumper with tomato sauce. *Oh no! Her best, and at that moment, only jumper!* She grabbed a kitchen cloth and dabbed at the offending orange splodges. *Okay, she should have called home earlier, but how was she to know Mum had been trying to reach her for hours, on her UK number, not her new French one?* And then her dad had been quite out of order suggesting Marcus was leading her astray! 'He's not!' she'd yelled. 'Quite the opposite. It was me who forced *him* to come here, besides, you forget, I'm nearly fifteen.'

Tatiana had stiffened. *How could she?* She'd waited, visualizing his pinched lips as the ominous silence at the other end had grown longer and longer until she couldn't stand it, and pulling a face at the receiver, had hung up. *Oh my God, now what have I done?*

She gave the pasta another stir. 'Louis, do *your* parents know we're here?' she asked, in a small voice.

'I didn't actually mention it...'

'So they'd mind?'

Obviously embarrassed, Louis looked away. 'Father wouldn't be minding, not at all, he thought you … *très charmante,*' he said, his eyes crinkling. Besides, he likes me to be independent. *Mais my mother,* she … is, how do you say it?' He threw his arms in the air. 'She is a very difficult person. She bosses my poor father about and tries to control my life, which I am detesting, so that's why I don't tell her anything unless I have to.'

Tatiana turned to him and with a wry smile said, 'Tell me about it! My dad's just the same. But one day it will change.'

'It will, but right now I'm having a terrible battle with her over college. I'm determined to study in America or England, only she argues all the time, demanding for me to attend the Sorbonne in Paris, just so I will be close to home! Can you imagine, when all I'm wanting, is to escape?'

'You *have* to stand up to her Louis,' said Marcus, with unexpected force.

'Oh don't worry, I do, and now I'm driving, she doesn't know what I do or where I go and that is really annoying her.'

After they'd eaten, they idled the evening away, huddled by the fire listening to Louis's CDs while Tatiana quizzed him about the family.

'Nothing is written, but *Grand-père* told me that two Lafonts lost their heads during the Revolution,' said Louis.

'*Two*?'

'Yes, Philippe and a woman.'

'Isabella?' gasped Tatiana.

Louis shook his head. 'No one knows who she was.'

'What happened to the bodies?' asked Marcus.

'I don't know about theirs, but most were thrown into

communal graves, unless the families were brave enough to risk collecting them.'

During this conversation the blood had drained slowly from Tatiana's already ashen face; it wasn't what she wanted to hear. If Isabella had been executed, then her final days would have been in prison in Paris, not here as she'd hoped. As waves of apprehension surged through her, she wondered why they were only learning this now.

'Well, I still think she's here,' she muttered, trying to convince herself more than the others. *Surely André or the Chevalier, could have brought their bodies home, couldn't they?'*

It was getting late when Tatiana and Marcus decided to test their nerves and resolve to find Isabella by sleeping in the room of the weeping woman. Marcus thought it a great idea, but as they were crossing the hall to go upstairs, a power cut plunged them into a total blackout.

'Louis!'

'Stay here, I'm finding a torch,' he said.

Alone and unable to see, Marcus edged closer to Tatiana. 'You okay?' he asked.

She nodded. 'Dad upset me earlier, but I'm fine now.' *That was a lie, but she refused to voice her terror.* They were still huddled together, waiting, when the moon, emerging from behind a cloud, illuminated the hall floor with windowpane shaped patches of silvery light.

'That's better,' said Marcus, in an over-loud voice.

'Hush, Marcus! You'll disturb the mice,' whispered Tatiana, as she tiptoed over to the window.

'Mice? What mice?'

Tatiana shrugged. 'This place must be full of them, and bats.'

When Louis eventually returned he was carrying candles. 'I couldn't be finding a torch, but these should do until the lights come back.'

'I hope so, 'cos I don't fancy sleeping in a haunted room in complete darkness. Do you, Marcus?'

'Well I'd rather not ... even with you there.'

'We'll wait then,' said Louis. 'What would you like to do? Coffee, tea, hot chocolate?'

'Music would be good.'

'That's not possible.'

'It is, the piano! And let's have yummy chocolate.'

Louis handed Marcus and Tatiana a candlestick and box of matches and left them to find their way to the music room while he returned to the kitchen. They crept along the passage with ever diminishing bravado, for, as they quickly discovered, the slightest movement made the candle flicker and menacing shadows to dart like cloaked phantoms around them.

'I so don't like this,' muttered Tatiana.

'We're nearly there,' said Marcus. But as he pushed open the heavy door, a draught caught the flame and blew it out.

'Bloody Hell!'

Marcus re-lit the candle and as Tatiana sat down, placed it on the piano beside her. She was halfway through singing a hastily improvised version of the poem when Louis came in with the drinks and, concealed by the shadows, stood listening.

'...mice in moonbeams on the stairs,

...bats flittering through the hall...'

'Your singing is beautiful,' said Louis, his voice as velvety as the darkness surrounding them.

'The words kind of echo this place,' she said, thinking that he looked pretty good too, all darkly handsome, his strong features accentuated by the candlelight.

'That tune ... it's a traditional folk song, *n'est-ce pas*?'

'Yes. Only I don't know the words, do you?'

'I used to, but now I am forgetting,' he said.

'Tati thought she'd made it up,' said Marcus.

'Your *maman* probably sang it when you were little, or you

may know it from Haydn's Eighty-Fifth, *La Reine*.'

'No,' she said, looking surprised.

'You should be hearing it then because it was *très populaire, 'top of the pops'* before the Revolution and Isabella would have known it well.'

'Do you have sheet music for it?'

'*Mais non*! It's a symphony.'

Tatiana had begun playing something more lively when Marcus looked out of the window and casually announced that it had stopped snowing. Tatiana immediately abandoned the piano and pressing her nose against the frosty glass, exclaimed, 'The snow's so beautiful in the moonlight, let's go out!'

'Not in the dark?'

'Yes. Now it's stopped, we can go to the maze ... in the moonlight ... together,' she murmured looking at him through her eyelashes.

'*Awesome*!' he said, grinning.

'You coming, Louis?' she asked, making Marcus frown.

'*Mais bien sûr.*'

Chapter 16

Moonlight Shadows

Everything outside had been mantled in a glistening blanket of snow rendering the slumbering garden barely recognisable. Walls, shrubs, benches had all been transformed into mysterious mounds, the entire landscape turned into a secretive mass of strange dust-sheeted shapes. It was ethereal and beautiful, but the depth of snow made walking difficult and progress towards the maze was slow.

'Isn't it wonderful?' cried Tatiana, twirling around. She loved the way the branches, crusted and bowed under their heavy burden, cast bar-code shadows across the paths as the three of them struggled through the shimmering moonlit drifts.

'*Attention,*' warned Louis, but too late, for Tatiana had taken one leap too many and disappeared over the edge of a buried step. Louis, with his impeccable manners went to help her up. She was about to grasp his extended hands, when she saw Marcus's body stiffen and his blazing eyes bore into Louis's back.

'I'm fine, thanks,' she said, and with a peel of girlish laughter, shook herself free.

'We'll leave footprints in the maze this time, so it'll be easier to get out,' said Marcus, thumping the snow off Tatiana's back.

'Better I tell you the system,' said Louis. 'It's very simple and works for most labyrinths. You place your left hand on the left hedge when you are entering, and keep it there, then following whichever way it goes, you'll arrive at the centre.'

'Wow, that's so easy!' said Marcus.

Tatiana hesitated. The thick layer of snow topping the symmetrical hedges made them look like slices from a surreal wedding cake. More flakes had lodged in the tiny crevices between the clipped branches, making them sparkle in the frosty light, but the interior, she knew would be blacker than a beetle on a dark night. The maze's dreamlike beauty was enticing, yet the thought of actually going inside was distinctly daunting. She didn't want to admit it, but she was nervous; that was until Louis noticed her dithering and took her gloved hand in his. For a moment she thought of resisting, but his grip was firm and reassuring; besides, Marcus had already gone ahead without her.

Marcus led the way; his fingertips trailing the icy hedge, forced him to keep close to the sides as they twisted along the paths. Apart from the snow creaking beneath their boots, they moved in silence, their warm breath clouding the air as they wound their way towards the centre. Occasionally the unruffled hush was punctuated by the dull thud of snow falling from branches, or the distant hoot of a lone owl.

Tatiana started. 'What was that?' she whispered, clenching tighter to Louis.

'I didn't see anything,' he said, pulling her closer.

'I *thought* … but maybe not, it's so dark.'

'Nearly there,' called Marcus, who was striding confidently ahead. 'It's so easy once you know how.'

'Ah yes, but it spoils the fun too, *n'est-ce pas*?' said Louis.

On reaching the middle, Marcus stopped and peered into the semi-darkness. The sarcophagus in the centre loomed vast and more mysterious than ever in its all-enveloping white shroud, while the freezing moonlight made the surrounding hedges stand out in hard relief against the unsullied snow.

'Now what?' he asked.

'We should shut our eyes and ask Isabella to appear – like we sort of imagine her here,' said Tatiana, doing her best not to catch Louis's eye.

'Ask her to come … is that what you said?'

'*Oui; et toi aussi,* Louis.' We all have a sort of connection to her, so if there's any chance of—'

Tatiana froze. Opposite them, sandwiched between two

perpendicular hedges stood a woman and child. How long they'd been there she didn't know, but as they stared fixedly at each other time appeared to stand still. Then as the woman evaporated into nothingness, the child raised his hand and pointing, ran towards them, passing straight through the sarcophagus before vanishing into the night.

'Mon Dieu!' spluttered Tatiana in an excited half-strangled cry. 'They're here, *I've seen her!'*

'Are you sure?'

'Yes, Isabella and the boy I saw earlier, only all dressed up.'

'In what way?' asked Louis.

'He was dressed like an adult in a velvet frock coat, breeches, buckle shoes and a hat covering his curly blond hair.'

As she described the boy, Louis slowly nodded.

'And that wasn't all,' said Tatiana, 'because before he vanished, he ran into the sarcophagus, why would he do that?'

'Must be a clue she's inside,' said Marcus.

'Tomorrow we'll look,' said Louis. 'Then we can be knowing for certain.'

'Oh I can't wait!' cried Tatiana doing a quick pirouette in the snow. But then she stopped. *Supposing it wasn't them?* The dreaded icy fingers of doubt were twitching at the very thought. *No, she mustn't think even think about it.*

Back at the chateau they huddled beside the dying embers of the kitchen fire thawing their frozen limbs and discussed the probability of it being Isabella.

'If it was her then we needn't sleep in the haunted room,' remarked Tatiana, wiping chocolate off her nose.

'You recognised her, *non*?' Louis asked, with an inclination of the head.

Well, I think so, although in real life I've only ever seen her portrait; but it has to be, we were all thinking of her, willing her to come.'

'Come off it, Tati, we hadn't got that far, we'd hardly even begun,' said Marcus.

'No, but the whole search was *for her,* and we *were* talking about her when,' she clicked her fingers, 'there she was.'

'And the boy?'

'I'm thinking he's Jean-Louis, the son who died,' said Louis.

'So *that's* who he is!' said Tatiana, turning to Louis in amazement. Marcus and Tatiana turned, eyebrows raised, staring at him.

'*How do you know?*' they said, in unison.

Louis jumped and blinking rapidly, spluttered, 'I don't ... your description, a picture maybe...' Looking decidedly disconcerted, he pulled himself up straight and frowning, continued brusquely, 'Your strange ideas seem to be catching, making me crazy, imagining things. But now it's late, let's find you both somewhere to sleep.'

Louis showed Tatiana to one of the formal bedrooms, one that on open days would be visited by the public. It was sparsely, if grandly furnished with little other than a four-poster bed hung with long blue brocade curtains, a marquetry night table, a small writing desk with spindly legs, and a scattering of up-right chairs. Louis drew the heavily draped curtains across the windows, blocking out what little moonlight there was. He then kissed her on both cheeks, and wishing her a good night, left. Tatiana kicked off her shoes and clambered into the chilly bed fully clothed. The moment she blew out the candle, she felt uneasy. It wasn't that she minded being alone in the strange room, or the acrid smoke still hanging in the air from the candle, it was something else keeping her awake, a feeling that something not very nice was about to happen. After a few minutes of sitting rigidly to attention, her knees up under her chin, she inched herself under the bedclothes. The bed gradually began to warm up and she'd relaxed enough to fall asleep when she was jolted to her senses by a sensation similar to drops of water trickling down her back. She knew what that meant, and much as she longed to find Isabella, right now, alone in the dark with nothing other than a box of matches and a snuffed out candle stub for comfort, wasn't her moment of choice. *If it's you with the missing teeth, please go away, but if it's you Isabella…* She clenched her teeth. *Could she send her away on her own, without Marcus? Well, there was only one way to find out.*

Her mind was still churning when the air around her started vibrating with an inaudible, yet discernable buzz. Her body tensed, and breathing heavily, she closed her eyes. And so she remained, straining for the slightest sound or movement from the surrounding darkness. After a while, she thought she must have nodded off, but wasn't sure, because when she opened her eyes to check, the room was no longer in total darkness, but filled with a diffused light that didn't seem to emanate from anywhere obvious. She was looking for a possible source when a shapeless grey blur appeared alongside the bed, making her jump. Determined not to turn away, she watched as the apparition gradually solidified into Natasha's welcome shape.

'Granny, it's you!' Tatiana cried. *What a relief, but now to quiz her before she vanished again.*

'Yes, I've been waiting for you to go to sleep so we can talk properly,' she heard her grandmother whisper.

'I was almost asleep when ... never mind, I'll try again, but please don't go,' she said turning over, and in a matter of minutes was fast asleep dreaming of her grandmother.

'Granny, when we needed your help today, why didn't you come?'

'I did. I've been here all along, trying to put thoughts into your head, but it's quite difficult without a body,' she protested.

'*Was* that Isabella in the maze?'

'Yes of course. I thought you'd realised she'd be there.'

'Well we were hoping she would be, but logically, it didn't make sense.'

'It took a great deal of effort for us to manifest those feathers, as a clue.'

'*You* dropped the feathers!'

'With the help of Jean-Louis, it was his idea and it was particularly difficult to arrange, especially three of them.'

'Surely Louis didn't need a feather.'

'Indeed he did. Although he may not realise it, he's just as involved in this as you and Marcus.'

'But if you knew she was here all along, why couldn't you have simply told me?'

'Because I didn't know for certain she'd be here. The last time I saw her she was in a very dark unpleasant place, maybe where she died, I don't know. Anyway now she's here you must seize the moment and release her.'

Tatiana nodded. 'But first, is this Jean-Louis, Lisette's brother?'

'Yes.'

'I wondered, because of what Louis said. But it doesn't matter – didn't he die long before Isabella?'

'He did. But unlike her, he isn't a ghost, he's simply materialised in a form she'll recognise in order to help. Jean-Louis's been trying to encourage her to leave, but without success. He's had trouble making her aware of his presence, although now she is beginning to respond to some of his impulses, it was he who prompted her to come to the maze tonight.'

'So, she's not trapped in the maze?'

'No, just visiting. She used to play with her children there in happier times, and now stuck in her twilight world, she sometimes goes there looking for you both, so you must act quickly before she drifts away again.'

'But how? Tell me ... *please*,' she urged, as Natasha's shape started disintegrating around the edges.

'There's a sense of her feeling guilty for not being there to take care of you, so forgive her – and follow your instincts.'

'Granny! Can't you help?'

'Don't worry, Jean-Louis and I will be there, giving whatever help we can.'

'More feathers?'

'I don't know yet. Wait and see!' she said, and laughing, evaporated along with the diffused light that had filled the room.

With her departure, Tatiana's dream changed and she found herself falling rapidly through clouds of white feathers, which transformed into giant snowflakes as she awoke to the piercing shriek of a peacock roosting on her windowsill.

Chapter 17

Haydn's Music

Tatiana noticed Louis was very quiet at breakfast the next day; he seemed pensive with a troubled look clouding his dark eyes. '*Ça va*, you okay?' she asked.

'*Mais oui,* but all your talk of Isabella and the Revolution made me have vivid dreamings last night,' he said.

'Can you remember them?'

'I am thinking so. I had trouble getting to sleep. Although I'm not understanding all your strange thinkings, I couldn't get them out of my head. I was wanting to dismiss them as fantasies, but something was telling me it wasn't that simple,' he said, his eyes searching Tatiana's face. 'And you puzzle me. Sometimes when you smile it's like looking at someone … *différente* … someone I already know and yet I can't quite be remembering … and then I'm forgetting you're so young. My feelings are all mixed-up. Anyway I did sleep; only it was restless with dreams.'

'Your dream, Louis,' said Tatiana, leaning across the table. 'Please tell us, it may be important.'

'How can a dream be important? Dreams are just … meaningless.'

'Mostly, yes, but sometimes they're different, real,' said Marcus.

'So tell, Louis, in French if it's easier, and I'll translate for Marcus.'

'Well, it must have been all this talk of Revolution, because I was there, in Paris. I was riding a horse as part of a military escort accompanying a horse-drawn cart or tumbril to the guillotine. There were many people in the cart including a tall arrogant-looking man and a young woman, both of whom I knew. Everyone had their hands tied behind their backs and some were so frightened, I could see them shaking. The tall man wasn't correctly dressed, just an open shirt with breeches and naked feet, I'd never seen him like that before and was shocked. The woman beside him was also half-dressed, and all of them must have been unwashed for there was a foul smell of sweat, urine and above all fear.' Louis paused, staring at the dregs in his empty coffee mug. Tatiana, unable to stand the suspense, touched his arm, prompting him to continue. He turned, an unfathomable look in his eyes, as he searched her face trying to break down the invisible barrier between then and now.

'What next?'

'We arrived in the *Place de la Concorde* where an excited mob were squabbling for the best viewing places to see the executions. It was then that I realised my uniform was but a disguise, so good that even the people in the cart didn't recognise me, and that I was part of an elaborate plan to save these two people. They should have been last to leave the cart, but something went wrong and their names were called first. Unable to help, I watched in horror, as the man, protesting the woman's innocence was led up the steps to the guillotine. People in the crowd were shouting, jeering and throwing rotten vegetables at him. I couldn't see what happened next, but heard the thud of the blade hitting the block and the cheer from the crowd as – as the man's severed head, blood spurting from the stump of neck, was held up for all to see. It must have been too much for the woman, because she fainted, and as she was hauled unconscious from the steps, I turned away.'

'Was she executed?'

'I don't know, I woke up. But before that, I was seeing you in the crowd,' he said, turning to Marcus.

Marcus's eyes lit up. '*Me!* Are you sure?'

'Yes. It was not *you*, but at the same time, I somehow knew it was.'

'Tati said something like that before, only she wouldn't tell me who I was,' Marcus said, pulling a face at Tatiana.

'And the executed man must have known you too, because before he was strapped down, he shouted, asking you to take care of his family, to get them out of France,' continued Louis.

'What *exactly* did he shout?'

'André! Take them to Russia.' See what your crazy stories are doing to me?'

'Louis! This is amazing.' You've just confirmed what I've been thinking. It's like you were remembering being... But, who were you and who were they?'

Louis shrugged. 'I don't know, but they were obviously aristocrats.'

'I bet it was Philippe and Isabella. And maybe she wasn't executed; perhaps you threw her across your saddle and galloped off with her like a knight in shining armour?' said Tatiana, becoming more and more excited.

Louis shook his head and frowning deeply, jumped up and made a great deal of noise filling the kettle and lighting the gas stove.

Tatiana had gone very quiet, trying to remember something eluding her from a recent dream, when Louis broke into her thoughts. 'Who is this André?'

'He was Isabella's cousin,' she said, looking pointedly at Marcus. 'A Russian, which would suggest the executed man was Philippe.'

'And the woman?'

'Well, there were only two possible Lafont women, Isabella and Cécile, because Lisette escaped ... didn't you Tati?' said Marcus.

Tatiana went rigid, her face contorted. *What did he have to say that for?*

'You were Lisette and Marcus was André? And now you are thinking I was living then too?' Louis said looking more and more puzzled. 'How are you knowing all this?'

'Because of dreams and—'

'Tati sees ... knows things, remembers...'

'Marcus!' yelled Tatiana as she saw a look of incredulity flash over Louis face. *Why did he always have to be so horribly up-front?*

But then Marcus added, 'Or perhaps it's just a genetic memory thing.'

'Genetic memory, what is this?' asked Louis.

'You know, your cells retaining the memory of the genes from which they're descended. After all you're both directly related so you could have the same genes, and remember the same things,' said Marcus brightly.

'Genes would seem quite logical to me, and something I could accept from a view point scientific,' said Louis.

'Good. Then will you help us rescue Isabella?'

'Before I can answer such a crazy question, you have to tell me what you mean by rescue? Why does she need to be rescued and from whom?'

'Not *from* anyone. It's a bit complicated. You see, she's stuck, doesn't know she's dead, that's what ghosts are ... the spirits of people who don't die properly, and we need to help her ... move on,' said Tatiana.

'So they have to be told they are dead and sent on their way to heaven, see?' added Marcus abruptly.

'*Non*. I do *not* see. *Et pourquoi*, why you? Shouldn't a priest to do this?'

'I expect a priest *could* do it, but you would have to convince your parents and a priest that it needs to be done, and they'd have to find her, and—'

Louis held his hands in the air. 'Okay, I am seeing the problem. You go ahead and if I can be helping then I will.'

'The only problem is how?' said Tatiana, looking apprehensively at Marcus.

'Like we did with the children. And what about Louis reading some prayers?'

'Good idea. The only trouble is, in my dream Granny said Isabella only *visits* the maze.'

'Then we'd better get on with it, before she goes back to … hell knows where,' Marcus was saying, when the telephone rang. Louise went to answer it.

Louis soon returned with the news that a thaw was forecast and his parents hoped to be back later that day. Tatiana groaned, this was really her last chance and they needed all the time they could get, but it did prompt her to call her mum. She'd been nervous of talking to her so was relieved when after assuring her that Louis was glad of their company, she'd relaxed about them staying for another day.

With breakfast over, they got ready to return to the maze. Muffled in as many layers of clothes as they could find, their pockets stuffed with anything they thought might be of use, including a bell, incense sticks, a variety of candles, and Louis's prayer book. Then with Louis clutching a crowbar, and Tatiana a small bunch of flowers, they set off for the maze. More snow had fallen during the night, and as they scrunched through the garden they came across bemused animals searching for food; blackbirds scratched for grubs amongst rotting leaves beneath bushes, whilst the normally elegant peacocks were rendered ungainly as their feet broke through the frozen crust in abrupt jolts.

Their footprints from the night before were still visible in sections of the west-facing paths in the maze, but the rest was still deep in virgin snow.

'It seems a shame to walk on it,' said Tatiana, reluctant to spoil the stark beauty of nature's handiwork.

'Come on, Tati, we can't stand here all day admiring the scenery,' said Marcus, giving her a playful shove.

Upon reaching the middle Louis swept the thick layer of snow off the top of the sarcophagus, wedged the crowbar under the lid and pushed. 'Now we are seeing what's inside.'

After more levering with the crowbar the boys managed to swivel the heavy lid far enough to allow them to see inside. The three of them hung over the edge, squinting into the dark interior. *'Rien!'* said Louis, as his torch beam revealed the sarcophagus to be empty.

'No skeleton, nothing!'

'*Quel dommage.*'

'It's a pity, but we didn't really expect…' Tatiana said, her voice trailing away.

'No, but we were *hoping,* after all her remains could have been moved here when they cleared the cemeteries in Paris.'

'So that's not good then,' said Louis, looking earnestly at Tatiana.

'Bones or no bones, we can still try and send her spirit away,' said Marcus.

After Louis and Marcus had replaced the lid, Tatiana took a candle out of her pocket and placed it on the top, but while she was fumbling for the matches, the candle toppled over and slowly rolled off. She plucked the candle out of the snow and replaced it, whereupon it did exactly the same again.

'Watch this,' she said.

'It slopes at this end,' said Marcus, who'd bent down for a better look. 'Can't be much though.'

'Probably subsidence,' said Louis. 'It must be *incroyablement* heavy and if the ground was being soggy that would cause it sinking.'

'Anyway, it's not that bad, use the big candle, Tati, that won't fall over.'

Tatiana placed a large candle on the top of the sarcophagus with four smaller ones at each corner, wedging them upright with compressed snow. Having done the same with some incense sticks, she sprinkled the surface with yellow petals plucked from a winter flowering jasmine she'd found in a greenhouse.

'What else have we got?'

'A bell, it's a bit feeble and tinkly, but it works,' said Marcus.

'And here's the prayer book and a bible,' said Louis, placing them beside the small brass bell.

Marcus lit the candles and incense and stepped back. 'What now?'

'I think we should close our eyes and concentrate on Isabella, try and imagine her here, ask Jean-Louis to bring her,' said Tatiana.

'Then?' asked Marcus.

'Wait and see.'

'We should say prayings. I have marked some that she would be familiar with,' said Louis.

'And I must tell her that Lisette was all right, in case she blamed herself for deserting her – by dying – or something like that,' muttered Tatiana, who was no longer sure about anything.

Marcus, Louis and Tatiana stood around the sarcophagus, their eyes closed, willing Isabella to appear. After ten minutes of silent meditation, Tatiana rang the little bell three times. Louis opened the prayer book and started to read, his strong clear voice resonating around the maze as he recited the prayers and incantations in faultless Latin. While Louis read, Marcus walked solemnly around the sarcophagus wafting the pungent smoke from the incense in all four directions. Then they stood still and waited.

After several minutes had gone by Louis whispered, 'Has anything happened?'

'Don't think so,' said Marcus. 'Perhaps we should try something else, not so heavy and serious.'

Tatiana had begun humming her tune, when Louis turned to her. 'That's it; you are giving me an idea. Wait here, I'm going to be fetching something.'

As Louis disappeared from sight, Tatiana suggested they try contacting Natasha while they were alone.

'Not wait for Louis?'

'No. It's too difficult to explain about having a grandmother in spirit who's helping us. I think all this ghost stuff is taxing him quite enough already.'

'Right then, now *really* concentrate this time.'

Some time later, Marcus and Tatiana were still standing with their eyes tight shut when Louis reappeared carrying a canvas rucksack.

'Music!' he said.

'*Music*? What music, Louis?'

'Wait and see.' And smiling mysteriously, he produced a portable CD player and mini speakers out of the bag. 'Sorry I was taking so long, I had troubles finding batteries, and then it took more minutes finding this *particulier* CD.'

'Hope it's not heavy metal or jazz,' quipped Marcus.

'Louis ignored Marcus and told them to shut their eyes and listen. 'I'm going to play the second track to see what you are thinking.' He pressed the start button, turned the volume to maximum and as the opening bars flooded the circle, stood back to watch the reaction on their faces. Almost immediately Tatiana's heart started to expand, while the heaviness in her mind lifted and her innermost self, her soul, was soothed in a way that no amount of words could possibly have achieved. As long-forgotten emotions started to surface, Tatiana's face brightened, her closed eyes tightening at the corners, her slightly parted lips opening into a broad smile, and all the while her body swayed to the familiar rhythm.

Meanwhile Marcus's demeanour was also changing; he'd pulled himself up to his full height, squared his shoulders, his head high and cocked slightly to one side. His face was concentrated, his hands twitching, until unable to resist, he succumbed and raising his arms, beat time in the air. Louis smiled and pressed stop.

Marcus scowled at Louis. 'Why did you do that?' he demanded.

'You liked it then?'

Tatiana gazed at Louis. 'It was my tune, only so much better.'

'It's Haydn's version. The second movement of his Eighty-Fifth symphony I was telling you about; Marie Antoinette's favourite music. So what do you think? Shall we be playing it for her?'

'Louis! That's such a brilliant idea!' said Tatiana, beaming at him. 'Play it all.'

'It's long.'

'That doesn't matter, we'll sit and enjoy it and it will be so beautiful that she's bound to come,' she said, doing a quick twirl before sinking into the snow.

'You can't do that; you'll be perishing. Marcus, come, help me bring some picnic chairs.'

Marcus followed Louis back to the chateau.

Tatiana liked being alone in the maze. The fragmented sunlight was making the frosty hedges glint, and there was something in the air, something more than just the sharp smell of snow. Was it a lurking sense of apprehension, or better, anticipation producing that tiny ray of hope that was melting the block of fear lodged in her heart? She couldn't tell. She only hoped Louis's idea would work. *But was she cold!* She was jumping up and down, stamping her feet, when Louis and Marcus returned. They unfolded the picnic chairs, set them in a semi-circle and Louis started the music, this time from the beginning.

'Tell me what I should do,' he said.

'Just empty your mind, let your imagination take over; visualise her, whatever comes, go with it, see what happens. That's what we do, kind of feeding the imagination, like daydreaming only much better,' said Marcus.

Louis, looked more and more bemused. 'I don't daydream.'

'Then how about watching for signs while Tati and I do the – the thinking business,' said Marcus, and fingering the fragment of ribbon still in his pocket, wondered if it could have been hers.

'The music, her music's bound to help,' said Tatiana.

Louis had brought a rug for her, and she was glad of it. Wrapping it around herself she snuggled down in the chair.

Tatiana watched as the candles burnt steadily in the still air above the empty sarcophagus, and wondered at the surreal situation in which they now found themselves. The residue of the spicy tang from the incense still lingered and the music filled the maze with joyous up-lifting sounds, surely this must be a setting tempting enough to lure the most miserable of ghosts out of the dark. She thrust her hands into her pockets, closed her eyes and tried to recapture the scenes from her dream when André's musicians had played this same music for Isabella. Was it possible for a ghost to hear music, see snow? Could something as transient as music reach through time and space to penetrate even the darkest of places? *'Oh my God! How beautiful is this?'* She sighed, hugging herself as the music swept over her, filling her with such exquisite joy and pain she wanted to laugh and cry all at once, while at the same time, having to fight the urge to jump up and dance. No wonder Isabella loved this music.

'Please, Jean-Louis, Natasha, *make* her come; let her be drawn in by the colours and vibrations of the notes,' she pleaded. Then for a second something in the air around her changed and in spite of not being able to see anything physically, she knew that someone had arrived. Clutching tightly to the box containing Isabella's hair, she went through every detail she could remember of her from the picture at home. The pale blue silken folds of her skirt pooling on the floor, the stiff, tightly fitting bodice, lace at the neck and edging the long sleeves, the wide pink sash around her tiny waist. She dwelt on each detail; even the sad look in her green eyes and the weird way her hair stood high above her head, all covered in white powder like icing sugar on a meringue.

'I shall talk to you in my mind, Isabella, so try and hear me. You were my mother; you brought me into the world, gave me your love, but it wasn't your destiny to protect me forever. As my mother I loved you, try and feel that same love now. Don't blame yourself for what happened, it was how it was meant to be. Now I'm begging you, dearest *Maman,* to come away from those dark days and re-join your family and friends who are waiting for you.'

A feeling of such peace had settled over Tatiana that she wondered if she were asleep. She opened her eyes a fraction; no, finding she was awake, she glanced at the others. Marcus looked asleep, although she was sure he wasn't. Louis she couldn't tell; he was hunched in his canvas chair, arms tightly folded and completely motionless apart from his facial expressions. What was he seeing, thinking? All sorts of emotions seemed to be flashing across his face, but feeling that she was spying on something private, she shut her eyes. For a moment she could still see him, and smiled to herself as his face started to transmute, changing subtly but decidedly into someone different. A man in his mid-twenties, of medium height and ruggedly handsome with long dark hair tied with ribbon at the nape of his neck. He was wearing a tightly fitting blue coat with cutaway tails, high collar and intricately tied white cravat. Still smiling, she stared at him, until the image vanished. She opened her eyes to sneak another look at Louis. *How confusing; they were so different, yet somehow the same. Was it possible that Louis had really been the Chevalier?*

The gentle touch of Louis's hand on her hair made Tatiana jump. She rubbed her eyes and disentangling herself from the rug, whispered, 'When did the music stop?'

'Much time ago; I thought maybe you'd fallen asleep?'

'I don't think so, what about you?'

'Yes, maybe, although in the beginning I couldn't stop thinking how funny to be sitting in the middle of the labyrinth, deep in snow, listening to Haydn. Never am I doing something like this before! Then I am watching how the candles on the sarcophagus makes the snow shining until their flickering made me need to close my eyes.'

'I wonder if Marcus is still—'

'No I'm not, I'm frozen.' Marcus stretched and stood up. 'Anything to report, either of you?'

Chapter 18

Linking the Pieces

Tatiana noticed that Louis kept suspiciously quiet while she and Marcus shared their thoughts on what had happened.

'I held the ribbon and while concentrating on the music, tried to imagine her in here, happy and laughing with her children. Then I visualised them playing hide and seek amongst the hedges, but the only strong image I got was of a large black and green scarab beetle emerging from beneath the sarcophagus. The scarab I felt sure was an omen and that she would appear, so every now and then I opened my eyes and mentally beamed light towards where you saw her, Tati,' he said pointing.

'How do you, "beam light"?' asked Louis.

'I just imagine aiming light sabres, like in space movies. Didn't you ever see *Star Wars*?'

'*Mais oui*, of course!'

'Well like that. Did you see her, Tati?'

'Not really; I started by sort of praying to her, but that didn't feel right, so I willed Natasha to come instead and bring Jean-Louis and Isabella with her.'

'And did they?'

'No, but I had the feeling we were being watched, like when you get that tingly, wet-cobwebby sensation all over, so I'm sure someone was here, only being broad daylight I just couldn't see them.'

'Maybe it's not necessary to see them physically, just knowing they're here could be enough,' said Marcus.

'So I sent out lots of love, like a great big white balloon filled with bright light and asked her to go into it. '

'And?'

'Nothing, except a really peaceful feeling,' she said. Then

noticing the excited expression on Louis's face, asked, 'And you, Louis, how did you get on?'

Louis hesitated. 'This sort of thing is so new, so alien to me that it's being difficult to explain.'

'Something happened, didn't it?'

He nodded. 'I think I must have gone to sleep because I had a strange dream, but when I woke up, I thought I was seeing the same woman from my dream standing by the hedge.'

'Louis!' gasped Tatiana. 'You *saw* her?'

'More than we did,' muttered Marcus. 'And *was* it, Isabella?'

'It's hard to know.'

'Think, Louis. Remember Isabella would have looked very different to how we imagine her, all dirty and rough after being in prison and ill.'

'I know, but this person seemed older, almost ugly with very short ragged hair looking like it had been hacked off with a blunt knife, and they were clasping something dark and fluffy, a wig, I am thinking.'

'Still could have been Isabella,' said Marcus. 'Her hair might have been shaved because of lice … but a dark wig? I've only ever seen pictures of people with fancy white wigs.'

Tatiana, trying not to scratch at the thought of lice, said, 'Are you sure it was a woman not a man?'

'No, how can I be certain? I was just thinking it must be the same person from my dream.'

'So what did you do?'

'I prayed for whoever it was, to go to a peaceful place full of sun.'

'And?'

'I imagined the person floating away, surrounded by thousands of white feathers, but I suppose they could have been snowflakes,' he said, noticing flurries of snow blowing off the tops of the hedges.

'Did they go?' asked Tatiana.

'I don't know, but no one was there when I opened my eyes.'

'Can you remember the dream?'

'Yes, it's very clear and … real!'

'Please tell us.'

'I can't, it was long and complicated and my English is not being good enough,' he said.

'Tell Tati, and she'll translate like she did before,' said Marcus.

Louis looked uncertain, until Tatiana nodded encouragement, when he began.

'The first thing I noticed was a dank musty smell, like the inside of the sarcophagus; then it changed to more like sewerage. I covered my nose with a cloth soaked in clove and cinnamon oil, but it hardly helped. Finally it became so strong I opened my eyes, or thought I had, because although my eyes were wide open, I couldn't see a thing, nothing. I'd never known such darkness and didn't like it. I tried blinking, but the smell and darkness stayed the same. I wanted to leave, but unable to see, I didn't dare move, instead I stretched out my hands and encountered a wall on one side and oozing straw on the ground!'

'I know that place,' murmured Tatiana.

'I had just shouted, "Mon Dieu! This is worse than a thousand hells," when I heard a woman's voice echoing through the darkness, her words interspersed with coughing. "So, Chevalier, have you really come for me, at last?"

'I still wasn't sure if I was dreaming or not, so I called out, "Can you switch on the lights?" Nothing more happened and I was wondering where the hell I was when a scraping sound, as of stone on metal, was followed by a guttering light, which became brighter as she shuffled towards me.'

'Where were you, Louis?'

'Wait, Marcus! Let Louis finish,' said Tatiana.

'Holding the candle up to my face, the woman said, "I don't know about *switch*, but I still have candles and the tinderbox left by Lisette and André." Then she asked me, if everyone was in place. I was a bit confused and didn't know what to answer,' said Louis, 'so I closed my eyes again and thought about what you'd both said about going with the imagination, allowing dreams to happen. When I opened them again things were different. Although I still felt like me, I wasn't me, Louis, but this other person, and he knew exactly what he was doing.

'The Chevalier took the candle from the Countess and helped her back to the pallet where she'd been lying. As she lay on the dank mildewy straw, he straightened her skirt, folded her arms on her chest and covered her head with the remains of her wig. "Yes," he said, "everything is prepared and the others in place waiting for my signal. It will be risky, but God willing we will make it out of here, away from Paris and out of France. So, Madame are you now prepared to die?"

'"I am," she said. "Anything to get away from this horrible place where I've known nothing but degradation and suffering; to be back with Philippe and my precious Lisette. So pray tell me how best to achieve this – this dying?"

'The Chevalier deliberated. Had no one told her that her husband had been executed, the chateau ransacked, and the rest of the family forced into hiding, or was she too sick and confused to remember? And if not, should he be the one to tell her? No, those horrors were best left until she was well again, but what about, Lisette? Should he explain how it was entirely thanks to her insistence that he was there now, attempting to rescue her, and what a truly remarkable, courageous and, dare he say it, very beautiful young lady her daughter had become during her absence? Perhaps not, for if God was with them, she'd be reunited with her soon enough.

'"You must remain just as you are, Countess, absolutely still. I will now wrap you in my cloak and summons the guard. Once he has verified that you are indeed as dead as I say you are, I will cover your head, carry you up the stairs, along the passage and away from here. We will have to pass through the main entrance where, if we are unlucky, the duty guards may summons an officer to sign a release paper. If that happens, remain limp, allow your jaw to drop open, don't breath and whatever happens don't blink. I will re-cover your face just as soon as possible."

'"I'll do my best," whispered Isabella, and as a weak smile brightened her gaunt and sallow face, he caught a glimpse of the beauty that she'd once possessed.

'The Chevalier carried Isabella, un-apprehended, through the prison's long dark corridors, stinking of fear, until reaching the main entrance gates, where as anticipated, they were stopped by Revolutionary guards, two of them, both shouldering muskets.

'"Papers!"

'"Here," said the Chevalier, handing his over, "the deceased's are with the authorities, whose permission I have to remove the corpse."

'Isabella was becoming increasingly heavy in his arms as, hardly daring to breath himself, he waited, sweating, while the guards inspected his papers; then without so much as a bored glance at the body, they were waved through. He exhaled. They'd made it, were out and Isabella was at last free. In the relative safety of the street beyond the prison gates, the Chevalier shifted Isabella to a more comfortable position, and was striding towards the waiting carriage with her when a blast of fresh, unsullied air caught Isabella unawares, making her cough, and cough and cough.'

Tatiana, who at the mention of the Chevalier and Isabella's names had become increasingly excited, gulped, but remained silent while she absorbed the implications of what Louis had said. *Oh my God, this is just brilliant.*

Louis, his eyes still shut, went silent leaving Tatiana in a ferment of anticipation, until she couldn't stand it a moment longer.

'Don't stop there, Louis! What happened next?'

'I was woken by pounding on my back and an explosion of

gunshots ringing in my ears to find I was staring at the sarcophagus, and as I said, amongst the guttering candle flames was the woman. Then I stupidly blinked to find she'd gone, so perhaps I was still dreaming.'

'Describe what she was like in prison.'

Louis explained how terrifying the darkness had been in her fetid cell until she'd lit the candle, when he'd seen her properly. How her clothes fell in loose folds over her emaciated body, and about the woman's jagged and distinctly greasy tufts of light-brown hair. He described her prominent cheekbones and how her blues eyes, ringed by dark circles, seemed huge in her sunken face, and assumed, after all the talk of Isabella being stuck in a dark place, that this must be her.

Tatiana looked hard at Louis; everything was beginning to fit into place. 'And did they get away?'

'Maybe.' Louis bent forward holding his head. 'When I felt the thumps on my back, I knew, in spite of there being no immediate pain, that I'd been shot. I'd fallen face down on the cobbles my body half covering Isabella's, as if shielding her; there was a rushing noise in my ears and a gurgling deep in my chest and I couldn't speak. I must have been half-stunned, because I was mesmerised by a trickle of blood snaking slowly between the cobblestones, not knowing if the blood was hers or mine. There was no movement from Isabella beneath me, until a small hand, the skin deathly white under months of imbedded grime, reached out from under the cloak, and I knew that injured or not, she lived.'

Louis stopped and looking up, stared long and hard at Tatiana. Stared with such a faraway expression on his face that she felt sure he wasn't seeing her, but someone else.

'Was that it?' she finally asked.

Startled from his reverie, Louis looked away. 'No, not quite,' he said, and as Tatiana went back to translating for Marcus, he continued.

'There were raised voices and shouts accompanied by boots pounding over the ground to where we lay. Rough hands seized me and as they hauled me from the ground, I could see further along the street to where a carriage stood waiting. An agitated looking man, pacing beside it, kept looking in our direction; then he cupped his mouth and yelled, "Can you make it?" With a motion from my head and flicking movements with my hand, I indicated for him to go. For a moment he hesitated, but then he opened the carriage door, evidently said something to the occupants, then sprang onto the driving seat, gathered the reins, and with a final lingering look in our direction, raised the whip to the horses' flanks. The last image I remember was the face of a distraught girl pressing her nose to the back window of the carriage as it sped away.'

'Louis, do you know who he … who you were?' asked Marcus jumping to his feet. 'It's really important you remember.'

'This other man felt like me, Louis, but wait! This was only a dream, it can't be important, so what are you getting excited about?'

'Don't you see, this was more than *'just a dream,'* you were remembering being someone else,' said Marcus.

'Yes, another lifetime, and we were all there!' added Tatiana, gazing at him through a veil of half-forgotten memories.

Louis sat down heavily forcing his chair legs deeper into the snow. 'Is this right? Nothing you say makes sense. How could you have been in my dream?'

Tatiana turned to Louis and smiling said, 'Because I have had very similar dreams, same people, place, everything. This was memory from past lives lived together, so please try and remember the man's name, not just his title of, Chevalier.'

'Well, she called me, "Chevalier",' he said. Then narrowing his eyes at Marcus, he suddenly grinned. 'Ah! I am beginning to understand this game of yours, the man standing by the coach was the same as the one in the crowd by the guillotine, you

Marcus, the one you said was called André … well, he called me Henri.'

Tatiana, overcome by a sudden giddiness, clamped her hands over her mouth. 'So you *were* the Chevalier Henri Pellerin, my father's most trusted and loyal friend, who I … er, whose daughter, Cécile was in love with.' Breathless, she turned to Marcus, her eyes glowing. 'We're all so connected!'

'Why is this? You must be telling me – at once,' Louis demanded, seizing her by the wrists.

'You were the Chevalier Henri Pellerin, who worked with Philippe.'

'How are you knowing all this?' he asked, looking from Marcus to Tatiana as they jumped up and down laughing and hugging each other.

'Yes, Louis, I'll explain, but first, the person you saw over there?'

'Was it Isabella?'

'How can I be certain exactly who it was?'

'You said she was holding a tatty black wig? Could it have been a dog? Isabella had a fluffy Pekinese.'

'Then yes. I'm thinking, for sure it was a small dog, but more important, than the dog, Henri called her, "Countess",' he said, grinning.

Tatiana let out an exaggeratedly long sigh. 'Phew! Thank you, thank you so much, Louis, you're just amazing. Somehow, without knowing it or even really trying, it was you, not us, who rescued her.'

Louis was digesting Tatiana's remark, when his face suddenly brightened. 'I am knowing why it had to be me,' he said. 'I was needing to finish what I was failing to do all those years ago – rescue her!'

'Yay! Of course, that's it!'

Marcus, Tatiana and Louis were later leaning against the

sarcophagus, grinning when Marcus who'd pressed a handful of snow into a ball and was tossing it from hand to hand, coolly remarked, 'You, as in Henri, were obviously killed, but what about her, if it wasn't her at the guillotine with Philippe, then who was it?'

'That's something we'll probably never know,' Tatiana was saying when Marcus interrupted.

'Well, as it was a woman, it had to be either Isabella or her stepdaughter, and since Cécile was at court with her father when the Revolution kicked off, she would seem the most likely.'

As Marcus was talking, Louis, who was becoming increasingly excited, flung his head back and smiled at Tatiana. 'Will you translate, because more of my guillotine dream is coming back to me?' Tatiana nodded.

He sat down, and holding his head in his hands, and with his eyes tight shut, started to speak. '*Of course* I knew the girl in my dream; she was Philippe's daughter! I remember how in the early, happy days, when Cécile had first come to court, we had often spent time together.' Louis stopped, and looked at Marcus and Tatiana, his face contorted with untold anguish. 'Now I am remembering how desperate Henri felt as he sat on his horse waiting for the signal that never came, and how he tried not to be sick when Philippe's head, his eyes still horribly open, fell into the basket. Also how he watched Cécile jump from the tumbril, only to trip on the ragged hem of her skirt, and how the bodice of her gown was ripped leaving her breasts exposed. It was terrible because I could see by the way she held the material together that, even though she was facing imminent death, she was embarrassed being *déshabillée* in front of her father, and me, Henri,' he said.

'So Henri and Cécile *were* in love?' said Tatiana, her spirits suddenly plummeting.

'What's this?' asked Louis frowning. 'Henri, in love with Cécile? No! That's not right, but perhaps it was the other way around. I'm thinking he was more than a little in love with her younger, more interesting sister.'

'*Not Lisette*!' exclaimed Marcus, glaring at Tatiana who was twirling around in excited circles.

'So many years ago we were all related, is that right?' asked Louis, looking to Marcus for clarification.

'Well, sort of,' he said. 'We know Isabella was Tatiana's mother back then, that I was a distant cousin of hers, André Imertinsky, a Russian, who we suspect was secretly in love with Isabella and that you, it now seems weren't a relation, but a family friend!'

'But I might have become one,' said Louis, his eyes flickering towards Tatiana.

'No you didn't,' retorted Marcus. 'You were killed, remember?'

Later, with the boys carrying the chairs and with Tatiana clutching the remaining bits and pieces, they were wandering back through the maze and had turned into the final passage leading to the exit, when ahead of them, seemingly waiting to leave, Tatiana saw a small boy in pale blue breeches tugging, with icy-white fingers, at the hand of a beautiful woman. She slid to a halt, her heart pounding, and was staring hard when the little boy smiled at her, revealing a gummy gap where his two front teeth should have been. Tatiana gasped and hot salty tears flooded her eyes blurring the image of Isabella and Jean-Louis as they evaporated into the misty air away from the restricting coils of the maze and the other dark places that had held her for so long.

Louis, Marcus and Tatiana were trudging through the thawing snow towards the chateau, when a silent flight of ghostly grey birds flew overhead.

'*Voilà!*' exclaimed Louis pointing. 'How about that?' Amongst them, its sun-tipped wings leaving no shadow on the ground, was one pure white bird.

'I don't believe it! What are you thinking, Louis?' whispered Tatiana.

'C'est Isabella. Non?'

'You think they're taking her away? That's such a beautiful idea, I love it!' she cried, and dropping her things in the snow, threw her arms around him. For a moment Louis seemed to waver, but then as she and Marcus grinned at each other, he wrapped his arms around her, hugging her so tight and for so long she thought he'd never let her go. As their cheeks touched, huge surges of emotion swept through her making her want to cry, not with tears of sadness, but of joy. Still in his arms, she looked up and recognised a similar, if somewhat confused elation etched across his face. Slowly and she could tell, reluctantly, he released her. '*Tati, tu est très adorable,*' he said, and she knew he was still smiling as she danced off.

'I kept my promise, Isabella's left and . . . ' She swung round and catching Marcus's eye, punched the air and yelled, 'She's free and guess what? *So am I.* Free at last from the insistent prodding of impish Jean-Louis's fingers.'

Louis and Marcus grinned at each other as Tatiana leapt ahead of them, sliding on the slippery slushy surface of the terrace singing a hastily improvised version of 'her' song.

'Tell them we came and found her here,
By a dense green hedge and snow-filled sky.
We beamed her light and she's moved on,
Flying heavenwards, on the wings of a bird'

Tatiana stopped at the end of the terrace and clasping her hands to her frozen cheeks, gazed back at the two good-looking young men walking towards her, and sighed. *What to do?* They were both so different, yet in many ways very similar; of course Louis was that much older, more sophisticated, and there was something, an unseen force pulling her to him, but no, it was too soon, she wasn't ready for Louis, not yet. She was still contemplating the boys, when Louis disappeared off to return the garden chairs to an outhouse, leaving Marcus to catch up with her.

Marcus, looking very serious, stopped right in front of her. For a moment he looked at her, impassive, unblinking and silent. *Was he cross with her because of the way she'd hugged Louis?* She couldn't tell what he was thinking and the uncertainty was making her heart beat faster and faster. She wanted to reassure him, but couldn't speak. *Why didn't he say something instead of just staring at her?* She was wondering whether to apologise, when he leant forward and removing a strand of sun-flecked hair from her face, tucked it behind her ear. Their eyes met, and still without uttering a word, he pulled her towards him and slowly lowered his head until their foreheads were lightly touching. 'Tati ... you're quite special you know,' he finally whispered. His words left her glowing with relief, and a happiness she hadn't felt in months, swept over her. Tatiana tilted her head back and with her lips brushing softly against his cheek murmured, 'Thanks, Marcus, thanks for helping me, and most of all for being you.'

Epilogue

Completing the Circle

Back in her grandfather's apartment, Marcus and Tatiana pored over the events of the previous few days. The fact that they still hadn't found Isabella's grave no longer mattered, the only thing of importance was that they'd fulfilled Granny Natasha's mission and Isabella had moved on.

'I suppose we'll never know where or how she died,' said Tatiana.

'Or where she was buried,' muttered Marcus. 'And I'm still puzzled by my image of the scarab beetle coming out from under the sarcophagus – I'd felt so sure we'd find her there.'

'Now she's free, do you think she'll reincarnate again soon?'

'I don't know, Tati, ask your grandmother,' Marcus was saying, when Tatiana's phone rang.

'*It's Dad!* I can't answer it.'

'Go on, you can't avoid him indefinitely.'

Grimacing at Marcus, she picked up her phone, holding it with her fingertips like a spider. 'Hello, Dad.'

'Tatiana, look I'm sorry if I upset you.'

'No, Dad, I'm sorry, *really* sorry, I was way out of line … I should never have hung up on you'

'Listen to me. I was so angry I didn't finish what I was saying, and you're right, you do need to be allowed to grow up, and with that in mind I thought I'd give you the opportunity to learn something about finance and budgeting—'

Tatiana balked; she should have seen this coming. 'Dad, my maths grades are—'

'Don't interrupt! I have decided to put you on a monthly allowance, not much, but enough. You'll be responsible for staying within your limits and I'll show—'

Tatiana was hardly listening she was so ecstatic. *'Dad! Oh wow!* Thanks.' *Independence at last!* She could hardly believe it.

Her mum was still fussing around asking endless questions about what they'd eaten, where they'd slept, if they'd been cold with no electricity, wanting to know every last boring detail, when her grandfather interrupted her.

'Did you find the bones you were looking for?'

'No actual bones, we've given up on those,' said Marcus.

'Thank goodness for that,' said her mum.

Tatiana, grinned mischievously at her grandfather and said, 'Better than bones, we found her ghost!'

'And it was *Tati's grandmother,*' said Marcus, looking pointedly at her grandfather, 'who asked her to finish what *she'd* been trying to do before she died.'

Tatiana's mum rolled her eyes. 'And what was that exactly?'

'To find and free Isabella from being stuck,' said Tatiana.

'And why couldn't you have told us this before?'

'Because you wouldn't have believed us, would you?'

Her mum didn't speak. *Oh dear, she could see Mum still wasn't comfortable with the idea of ghosts.* 'Don't worry, Mum, everything's fine.'

Her mum sighed. 'Maybe here, but what about when we get home?'

'Trust me, Mum, everything will be back to normal, including the central heating in the drawing room.'

Jacques, his eyes brimming, got to his feet, shuffled over to Marcus and placing both hands on his shoulders, said, 'I do believe you. But tell me, where is Isabella's ghost now?'

'In heaven, probably with Natasha! And guess what finally made it happen? Music!'

'What music was that?' asked her gandfather, his eyes twinkling. 'Not your singing, Tatiana?'

'Not quite, it was Haydn's Eighty-Fifth.'

Her grandfather nodded quietly and although her mum's eyes flew to the ceiling and back yet again, she didn't utter a word. Later that evening her grandfather put the same piece of music on his old record player and sat back in his chair beating time with his fingers.

'Your grandmother was also very fond of this music, pity she didn't hum it on one of her trips to the chateau, might have saved everyone a lot of trouble,' he said. 'And if you're here now, Natasha, I hope you're listening.'

It was the early hours of the morning when Tatiana awoke to a semi-conscious state. The greenish-grey light edging the blind told her it was much too early to get up. She needed to go back to sleep, and was turning away from the window when she became aware of a presence in her room. She stiffened; she'd had more than enough of ghosts for the moment, but all the same she couldn't help checking. And sure enough, through half-closed eyes, she saw a shadowy form hovering by the end of her bed.

'Granny?' Her pulse was racing as the enigmatic blur slowly took on the figure of her grandmother.

'Of course, who did you think I was, Isabella?'

'No, but I can hardly see you. You're transparent like cellophane, with your body all muddled-up with the bedpost, my socks, the wallpaper and…' she was saying, when the air in the room started vibrating. 'Are you laughing at me?'

'Just a little, you make me sound so funny,' her grandmother said.

Tatiana, not sure whether it was funny or not, tittered nervously. 'So, has she gone?'

'Yes, but it will be easier if you close your eyes and we continue our conversation telepathically. That's why I've come, to thank you, all three of you, and to tell you she's moved away and met up with old friends already. For you and Marcus this has been a bit of a game, albeit at times a frightening one, but releasing a trapped soul, allowing them to continue their evolutionary journey is the kindest thing anyone can do. If only more people understood the importance of freeing these trapped spirits, then haunted houses would no longer have frightening entities scaring people and those lost souls could move on to better things.'

'I hope this doesn't mean you're going to send me on more ghost hunts?'

'No. Don't worry, you've done more than enough ... for the moment.'

Tatiana sighed, she really didn't fancy any more missions of that kind; however, she couldn't help thinking that if it hadn't been for her granny and Isabella she might never have met Louis.

'In the end it was Louis who made the final connection, wasn't it? Marcus and I were quite surprised by that.'

'For you, yes, not for me though, because you all go back a long way together, and although he doesn't yet know it, Louis has a spiritual understanding every bit as deep as yours.'

'Will he ... do you know if one day we...?'

'I know what you want to ask me and I can't answer, humans have free will, meaning anything can happen.'

'Then what about Isabella, will she come back soon?'

'Probably not for a while, but hopefully we'll all meet up again one day.'

'When we were all together during the Revolution, you were Henriette weren't you?'

'Of course, but you knew that. Now before I go I want you to do one more thing for me.'

'Granny! Not again!'

'It won't be so bad this time; just tell your grandfather I enjoyed listening to the music with him tonight; tell him that love never dies and that I love him more than ever. That's all.'

Marcus, Tatiana and Louis arranged to meet once more before the holidays came to an end. They'd agreed to return to the

Louvre to have a look at some of the galleries they'd missed before, but first they were going to pay another visit to the obelisk in the *Place de La Concorde.*

'You know, I've never seen this plaque to the dead of the Revolution,' said Louis.

'It's hardly surprising,' exclaimed Tatiana. 'It's so insignificant, you could easily miss it.'

'I've driven past hundreds of times, of course, but never stopped. It's so easy not to do things in your own country, things that tourists do automatically,' he said, looking somewhat shame-faced.

'Well now you're here … again and this time on your feet,' said Marcus, with a crooked grin.

'*Mon Dieu*! If you're right, if that dreaming was true, then I *have* been here before,' and looking up at the obelisk towering above them, the gold pyramidion peak glinting in the wintry sun, he pulled his coat tighter around him. 'You'll never be believing it, but somewhere else I've never been is the Eiffel Tower.'

'Neither has Marcus and Mum keeps on about it being a *must* before he leaves,' said Tatiana.

'Then we shall visit that too, but first, the Louvre.'

Before they left the obelisk Tatiana placed a posy of jonquils she'd been clutching all morning on the brass plaque at the base. 'A bit late perhaps, but these are for Philippe, Isabella, Cécile and all those forgotten souls of the Revolution,' she said.

Back in the Louvre they were warming up with hot cappuccinos in one of the cafés before starting out round the galleries when Louis told them that once the snow had melted he and his father had inspected the sarcophagus and had indeed found signs of subsidence at one end, and he thought Marcus would like to know there was a noticeable hole in the ground as if some small creature was living there.

'I told you I saw a beetle,' said Marcus.

'And, I found this in the library at home,' said Louis, producing an auction catalogue from his pocket. Opening it at a dog-eared page, he handed it to Tatiana. 'Could this have been you?'

Marcus and Tatiana scrutinised a photograph of a miniature painting of two young girls. It was no more than three inches long, painted on ivory, and perfect in every detail. Underneath the photograph was the caption, *Thought to be, Cécile and Lisette, daughters of Count Philippe Lafont.*

'Where did this come from?' exclaimed Tatiana.

'Father has many old sale catalogues, he's always looking if by chance family pieces come up for auction.'

'Where is it? Did he buy it?'

'I'm guessing not.'

'Why not?'

'Tati, I don't know, the catalogue's from the eighties, maybe he was being out-bid or couldn't afford it.'

'So somewhere it still exists.'

Tatiana pored over the picture, examining every detail. The eldest girl must have been about thirteen, while the younger couldn't have been more than six or seven. The elder had dark blond hair, the younger, sandy fair hair and both had blue eyes, but the thing that immediately attracted Tatiana's attention was the younger girl's dress. It was pale blue silk, trimmed with a double row of tiny dark blue bows down the front of the stiff bodice.

'Look, Marcus, blue ribbons – where's that piece you've got, could it be the same?'

'I'd hoped it was Isabella's, but if it was off Lisette's dress, then, it must be yours,' he said, and pulling it from his coat pocket held it out to her.

'No, you keep it,' she said.

'What do I want a bit of old ribbon for?' said Marcus, hurriedly returning it to his pocket.

'I'll photocopy the picture and post it to you, Tati. Now let's go,' said Louis, getting to his feet, 'for I'm thinking the miniature might possibly have been bought by a museum.'

'You mean it might be here?'

'I don't know, but after the events *extraordinaire* of the last few days, I'm believing anything's possible,' said Louis.

Four months later, when spring came, the last pieces of the puzzle finally fell into place. Tatiana's dad was helping her solve a problem with her maths homework when her iPhone buzzed in her pocket.

'Thanks, Dad,' she said, and giving him a quick kiss on the cheek, shot back to her room. It was a text from Louis telling her to phone. He had news.

Tatiana called immediately. He wanted to tell her that he was coming to England for a couple of weeks. 'I have interviews at two of your universities,' he said.

'*Louis!* Don't tell me your mum agreed?' she said, in French.

'It was being a bit of a struggle, but yes, in the end I won! But there's more.' He then told her that when workmen had moved the sarcophagus to investigate why it was sinking, they'd discovered a grave beneath, containing two coffins one on top of the other.

'*Isabella*!' Tatiana cried.

'Mais non,' said Louis. 'One of he skeletons has been identified as a man in his forties and the other, that of a teenage girl. Not only that, but neither of the sculls were attached to their bodies.'

'Philippe and Cécile then?'

'Yes. And something strange; in the girl's coffin was a small wooden box and inside, wrapped in fine cloth and bound with blue ribbon, was a keepsake - an entwined lock of two differing tones of fair hair.'

Tatiana smiled.

Acknowledgements

My thanks to Chris Waters, the late Kate Jones, Sandra Glover, Hannah Sheppard, Noga Applebaun, Sarah Stewart, Shelley Instone and all the team at JHP. But most of all to the unwavering support of my family and stalwart readers, Robert Tainsh and my daughter Alexi who have given up so much of their valuable time reading.